Lila was angry. "Come on, Andrea. Are you trying to say you don't have any sway over Jamie?"

"That isn't the point," Andrea said coldly.

"Maybe you don't," Lila added with a pout. "Maybe he doesn't even listen to you. Although if I were you, that would bother me. A lot. After all, you *are* his girlfriend."

Andrea stared at Lila. At first, she thought she hadn't heard her right. Then she started to laugh.

"What's so funny?" Lila snapped. "We all know the truth now, so don't think you can deny it."

"What's the 'truth,' Lila?" Andrea asked, her laughter subsiding and her anger taking over. "That Jamie is my *boyfriend*?"

"Well, isn't he?" she asked.

Andrea got to her feet. She could feel a dull throbbing in her head. Answering Lila right then was a little bit like answering every kid who'd ever wanted to know who Jamie Peters was to her. "Lila, listen. It's none of your business who Jamie Peters is to me!"

Bantam Books in the Sweet Valley High Series
Ask your bookseller for the books you have missed

SWEET VALLEY HIGH

ROCK STAR'S GIRL

Written by
Kate William

Created by
FRANCINE PASCAL

BANTAM BOOKS
NEW YORK · TORONTO · LONDON · SYDNEY · AUCKLAND

RL 6, IL age 12 and up

ROCK STAR'S GIRL
A Bantam Book / February 1991

Sweet Valley High is a registered trademark of Francine Pascal

Conceived by Francine Pascal

Produced by Daniel Weiss Associates, Inc.
33 West 17th Street
New York, NY 10011

Cover art by James Mathewuse

ISBN 0-553-28841-5

Published simultaneously in the United States and Canada

Bantam Books are published by Bantam Books, a division of Bantam Doubleday
Dell Publishing Group, Inc. Its trademark, consisting of the words "Bantam
Books" and the portrayal of a rooster, is Registered in U.S. Patent and Trademark
Office and in other countries. Marca Registrada. Bantam Books, 666 Fifth Avenue,
New York, New York 10103.

PRINTED IN THE UNITED STATES OF AMERICA

OPM   0 9 8 7 6 5 4 3 2 1

Dedicated to Valerie Sylvestre

One

"Hey, Liz!" Enid Rollins exclaimed, hurrying into the girls' locker room and dropping her bookbag onto the bench. Her green eyes were shining with excitement. "You'll never guess who I had lunch with today."

Elizabeth Wakefield grinned at her best friend's infectious enthusiasm. "Let me try," she said, scanning Enid's face for a clue. "Someone cute, funny, available—and male?"

Enid laughed. "Nope. Try again."

Elizabeth opened her gym locker, slipped off her navy-blue cotton sweater, and reached for her gym clothes. "I'm all out of ideas. You know I'm brain-dead by last period."

1

Enid gave her a reproachful look. "Does that mean you might actually consider cutting back on one or two of your extracurricular lives?" Enid had been teasing Elizabeth lately for taking on too much responsibility at *The Oracle*, the school paper. But Elizabeth was devoted to writing. She often thought of becoming a professional writer, and even though her schoolwork and her longtime boyfriend Todd Wilkins were priorities, she always made time to perfect her craft.

"You know me better than that!" Elizabeth exclaimed. "But don't keep me in suspense," she added with a smile. "Who was your mysterious lunch date?"

"It wasn't a date. If it had been, I wouldn't have been able to hold out till last period before telling you." Enid had recently broken up with Hugh Grayson and was more than a little interested in meeting someone new. "No, unfortunately this happened to be a girl. The new girl who's just moved here from New York City, Andrea Slade."

"Really!" Elizabeth leaned forward to lace up her sneakers, her blue-green eyes brightening. "I was going to introduce myself to her today, but I got sidetracked." Elizabeth had learned about the new girl when Penny Ayala, editor

2

in chief of *The Oracle*, handed her a list of new students and teachers, fresh material for "Eyes and Ears," the gossip column Elizabeth wrote. "She's a junior, right?"

Enid nodded. "Yep. I rescued her from the clutches of Bruce Patman," she continued. "Poor girl. She was sitting there all by herself at one of the lunch tables, completely defenseless, and he pounced on her. She obviously has good taste, though. She was grateful when I came over and sat down with her."

Elizabeth laughed. Bruce Patman had the biggest ego in all of Sweet Valley High. His parents were incredibly wealthy, and between his handsome appearance and his shiny Porsche, he thought he was God's gift to girls.

"If she saw through Bruce's charms that quickly, she *must* be pretty sharp!"

"I liked her a lot right away." Enid was enthusiastic. "She's very friendly, and she's so excited about living in Sweet Valley. Every little detail seems to blow her away."

"Well, this *is* a great place to live," Elizabeth reminded her friend. "Who could ask for more? Perfect weather all year round, gorgeous beaches—"

"Maybe you should write brochures for the local Chamber of Commerce," Enid teased.

"But, seriously, Andrea was excited about living in a small town—where people can get to know everyone else."

Elizabeth shared that feeling, too. Walking out to the playing fields with Enid, she felt a new appreciation for the familiar schoolyard, the flower-lined patios shaded with lovely old trees. Out on the fields, dozens of girls were lining up to sort into two teams for softball.

Elizabeth felt a twinge of empathy for Andrea. It must be hard to move to a new school in the middle of the year.

"Andrea must be having a tough time, not knowing anyone at school," she told Enid. "New York is a long way off, and it can't be an easy adjustment."

Enid nodded. "Well, she doesn't seem sorry to have left New York. But you're right, I'm sure it isn't easy—even for someone as friendly as Andrea. That's why I thought of asking her to join us at the beach Saturday."

"Great idea!" Elizabeth's eyes lit up. "Did you ask her already?"

"No—but here she comes." Enid tipped her chin toward the bleachers. "I wonder what she's doing here this period."

Andrea Slade was even prettier up close than Elizabeth had judged from her one glimpse of her the week before. She was slender and tall, with a wonderful mop of blond curls cascading down to her shoulders. Her blue eyes were wide-set and fringed with dark lashes, and she had a lovely peaches-and-cream complexion.

"Hi, Enid!" Andrea said breathlessly, hurrying up to join them. "I just got switched into this gym class. They're still working on my schedule down at the office, trying to make sense of what credits can be counted from my last school." She smiled curiously at Elizabeth.

Enid quickly introduced them. "This is Elizabeth Wakefield. Liz, Andrea Slade."

Andrea's smile widened. "Great! That makes two people I've met today. I'm not sure I count Bruce as a 'person'."

Elizabeth and Enid both laughed. Elizabeth instantly liked the new girl. She seemed fun, independent, and a little different from the new students Elizabeth met through her work for *The Oracle*. Maybe it came from living in New York. Andrea also seemed a little older and more sure of herself than most of Elizabeth's friends.

The gym teacher blew the whistle, and for the next forty minutes Elizabeth was too preoccupied with softball to speculate about the new

5

girl. But walking back to the locker room after class, Enid broached the subject of the beach.

"Andrea, have you had a chance to see much of Sweet Valley yet?"

"No, not really. We're still unpacking at home," Andrea explained. "I've probably seen more of the inside of the school administration office than anything else!"

"We were wondering," Enid continued, "if you wanted to come to the beach with us this Saturday. You know, check out the local sights and everything."

Andrea grinned. "I'd love to. I can already tell that having a tan is an absolute necessity here. And I've still got my East Coast pallor."

"Great!" Elizabeth said. "I'll tell you what. Why don't I pick you up? My car's a squeeze for three, but if you don't mind that, Enid and I can give you a full-scale tour."

"You know, I forgot to ask which part of town you've moved to," Enid added.

Andrea hesitated. "How about if I meet you at the beach? Our house is a real mess. We can barely find the front door with all the boxes scattered around."

"Sure, that's fine. Where should we meet, Enid? At the lifeguard's stand or at the concessions?"

They agreed on a meeting place and explained exactly where on the beach Andrea should look for them. "You may think you're in the middle of Manhattan. That's how crowded the beach can be on a Saturday," Enid joked.

After Andrea headed off to her locker to change, the two girls exchanged smiles. "Isn't she great?" Enid said warmly. "I think it's going to be a lot of fun having her in our class."

"Yeah, I think so, too," Elizabeth said. "She's really easy to be with. I get the sense there's nothing phony about her. She is who she is, you know what I mean?"

Enid nodded in agreement. "Something tells me that you and I have just made a fabulous new friend."

Elizabeth had barely opened the front door of the pretty split-level home where the Wakefields lived when Prince Albert, their golden Labrador retriever, shot out at her, barking with excitement.

Elizabeth laughed. "Calm down, Prince."

"That dog's been going berserk all afternoon," Jessica complained, wandering out into the hallway with a compact disc in her hand.

"Well, hello to you, too, Jess," Elizabeth said,

pretending to be annoyed with her twin's cool greeting.

Actually, Elizabeth enjoyed catching a glimpse of her twin sister off-guard. It was like looking in a mirror, Elizabeth thought. She and Jessica were identical down to the tiniest detail. Both had slim figures, and they could easily share each other's size-six clothing. Both had long, California-blond hair, eyes the bluish-green of the Pacific Ocean, and beautiful smiles. They were often mistaken for each other, and there were times when they had used that fact to their advantage.

But anyone close to either Jessica or Elizabeth could tell who was who in an instant. For one thing, Elizabeth wore a watch, and Jessica did not. Jessica went by what she called "Jessica Standard Time," which Elizabeth preferred to call "late." When it came to style, Jessica tended to go for whatever was new, and her clothes and jewelry reflected the very latest trends. Elizabeth, on the other hand, chose things that were more classic and traditional. Elizabeth was the older of the two by four minutes, and those minutes, as she often reminded Jessica, sometimes felt like light-years!

Elizabeth took her work and her friendships seriously, unlike Jessica, who went through interests and boyfriends almost as quickly as she went through clothing styles.

Jessica thrived on being in the limelight. That was one reason she loved cheerleading—it put her right out there on center stage. Her closest friends craved attention and excitement almost as much as she did, and sometimes Elizabeth got the distinct impression that Jessica thought Elizabeth and Enid were too boring and conventional.

But despite their differences, the twins were very close. Elizabeth would have loved to tell Jessica all about Andrea Slade right then, but Jessica was grabbing her denim jacket, apparently on her way out.

"Where are you going?" Elizabeth demanded. A warning bell went off in her head. "Isn't it your turn to help with dinner?" The twins' parents both worked long hours. Ned Wakefield was an attorney, and Alice Wakefield was an interior designer. Both Jessica and Elizabeth were supposed to help out as much as they could, especially now that their brother Steven was away at the nearby state university. But when it came to splitting chores, Jessica had an extraordinary way of making her share smaller and smaller.

"Liz, could you help me out this one time?"

Jessica pleaded. "I promised Lila I'd come over. She's got this amazing compact disc player her father got her in Japan, and Jamie Peters's brand-new album just came out. I picked it up at Records Plus at the mall. I've absolutely *got* to hear it right away!" She showed Elizabeth the disc, still wrapped. Jamie Peters was featured on the cover, holding a microphone and wearing sunglasses. His shoulder-length blond hair was pulled back in a ponytail. He was wearing a tight T-shirt, which emphasized his lean, muscular arms.

Elizabeth laughed when she saw the title of the album—*Pride*. "Pretty appropriate title for a rock star like Jamie Peters," she commented.

"Jamie Peters is simply the greatest male vocalist of the entire decade." Jessica defended the rock star. She fixed her gaze on the cover. "He's *so* gorgeous!"

Elizabeth laughed. "Well, I can see that helping out with dinner can't possibly compete with Jamie Peters. I'll take over for you tonight, Jess. But remember, you owe me one."

Jessica nodded, still in another world. "He's got this song on here called 'Doing It All for You.' I've heard it on the radio a few times. It's incredible. He doesn't use any backups or instrumentals or anything. And his voice gets really low and sexy for about eight bars. I can't remember all the words, but it's something like, 'Whatever you say, whatever you think is true . . . whatever it is, girl, I'm doing it all for you.' It's the sexiest song I've ever heard."

Elizabeth shook her head. "I'm sure I'll hear it soon," she said, leaning down to pat Prince Albert on the head.

Elizabeth liked Jamie Peters, too. In fact, Todd had two of his albums. But Jessica always had to turn *liking* into *adoring*. That was just the way Jessica was. She didn't just get interested—she got obsessed.

And Jamie Peters was clearly her latest obsession!

Two

"I can't stand it!" Lila Fowler cried in mock anguish, brushing her light brown hair out of her eyes as she stared down at the cover of the latest issue of *Rock and Roll* magazine. "Jamie Peters has got to be the sexiest man alive. Look at his eyes! Look at that cute little cleft in his chin."

"Listen to yourself, Lila," Amy Sutton said in her most critical voice. "You sound like a lovesick baby. Only teenyboppers get crushes on rock stars!"

Lila gave her a cold stare. "Who says I have a crush on him? I just happen to think he's drop-dead gorgeous, that's all." She jumped up, took the new disc out of its cover as if it were made of eggshells, and placed it gently in the disc player.

"I think it's silly, making such a big deal over someone just because he's famous." Amy made a face. Her mother was a sportscaster at a local TV station, and Amy liked playing up the fact that she was used to seeing stars all the time. She knew this kind of remark always got to Lila.

"I just happen to like his music, that's all," Lila said imperiously, as she turned up the volume.

Jessica settled back against one of the sumptuous pillows that were strewn all over Lila's bedroom floor. She wasn't going to let her friends' petty argument spoil her afternoon.

Lila's bedroom swelled with the opening notes of Jamie Peters's first song, "Little Girl." Neither Jessica, Amy, nor Lila made a sound as they listened to the lyrics. Jamie Peters's trademark was his deep, sultry voice, a voice that sounded to Jessica like a mixture of velvet and gravel.

"He's amazing." Jessica sighed when the song was over. "Lila, give me that magazine a second," she commanded.

Lila looked reluctant. "Wait a minute, will

you? I'm *reading*," she protested, holding up the article entitled "Jamie Peters—Who Is the One He's 'Doing It All For'?" A full-page photo of the rock star showed him leaning up against a brick wall, arms folded, a shy grin on his handsome face.

Even Amy seemed to soften when she saw that picture. "OK, I admit it. He's gorgeous," she said, twisting a strand of blond hair around a finger. "What does the article say about him? How old do you think he is, anyway?"

"Twenty-five," Jessica said promptly.

"No way," Amy corrected. "He's probably about forty. Look at those little wrinkly lines around his eyes. That's no twenty-five-year-old!"

"OK, maybe thirty, or thirty-five, max." Jessica guessed again.

"Stars can make themselves look any age they want to," Lila insisted. "Daddy was telling me that the last time he was in L.A. on business, he went into this health club to work out, and all the men were having stuff put on their skin to take away wrinkles."

"That's gross," Amy said, wrinkling her nose. "I can't see Jamie Peters ever doing something like that."

Jessica yanked the magazine out of Lila's

14

hands and rapidly scanned the print on the page before her. "See? It says here that Jamie's trying to get into films and out of the music industry. 'Could a switch into movies mean a cross-country move for East Coaster Jamie Peters? When *Rock and Roll* magazine asked him, all we got out of him was a 'Yeah, maybe. I like California. I wouldn't mind trading East Coast winters for perpetual sunshine!' "

"California!" Lila cried. "Maybe he'll move right here, to Sweet Valley!"

Amy gave her a look of sheer impatience. "Lila, get real," she admonished. "Why on earth would someone like Jamie Peters want to move to a little town like Sweet Valley? This is a town for families, not for sexy singers." She shook her head. "He'll probably move to Bel-Air or Beverly Hills," she added knowingly.

"You think you know everything," Lila sniffed, pulling the magazine back from Jessica. "I don't see why he couldn't move here. Sweet Valley's a great place to live, and it isn't far from L.A. Besides, some stars happen to like privacy."

Jessica could tell a fight between her two friends was brewing. It would not be the first time that Lila and Amy had squared off, and frankly, Jessica did not want to get in the middle of one of their squabbles. "Tell me more about what the article says," she said to Lila, hoping to change the subject.

Her strategy worked. Lila turned the page, and all three girls huddled together to have a look at the next photograph of Jamie. This one was even more spectacular than the last. On this page, Jamie was in his recording studio in New York, a pair of sunglasses pushed back on his head. A tight white T-shirt was rolled up at the sleeves to reveal well-defined arm muscles. One hand lay confidently on his electric guitar, and he faced the camera with an expression of smoldering defiance.

"Wow," Jessica breathed.

"He's incredible," Amy seconded.

"Hey, look." Lila pointed to the two columns of print on the next page.

Rock and Roll interviewers had a hard time getting to know the real Jamie Peters, the private side of the very public star,' " Lila read. " 'We talked for hours about his new album, *Pride*, and he was happy to answer all our questions about his music— where he's been, where he's heading. But when it came time to delve deeper, we could sense his mood change.

We asked him about the first song on his new album, "Little Girl." Was there a special woman in his life?

We could tell the question disturbed him. Jamie Peters is famous for keeping his personal life under wraps. All we were able to glean from him were the most basic facts. He married his childhood sweetheart, a beautiful singer named Karen Ross, with whom he cut an album the year they were married. Twelve years ago Karen was killed when her private jet crashed in the Adirondacks. Since then, Jamie Peters has been a different man. When we asked, all he'd say was that yes, there's a "special girl" in his life. And all *Rock and Roll* magazine can say is, whoever she is, she sure is *lucky*!

"You can say that again." Lila sighed.

"I don't believe it," Jessica moaned. "Why do all the really gorgeous guys have girlfriends already?"

Amy shook her head. "I can't *believe* you two! What do you think, if he happens to be free, you could just call him up and ask him out? You guys need to get your heads out of the ozone!"

"Imagine being Jamie Peters's girlfriend,"

Lila mused, ignoring Amy's comment completely. "I bet she goes around the world with him on tour."

"Yeah, and he writes her special songs all the time." Jessica's eyes were bright with excitement. "Can you imagine what it must feel like, driving your car somewhere, turning on the radio, hearing a song like 'Doing It All for You,' and knowing Jamie Peters wrote it for *you*?"

"You guys aren't very realistic about the way songs get written," Amy put in. "How do you know he even wrote those lyrics? Maybe he collaborated with someone else."

Lila glared at her. "Since when do you know so much about music, Amy? You don't know the first thing about it!"

Amy rolled her eyes. "Yeah, well, tell me *you* do."

Lila looked really angry now. "I happen to know a lot more about it than you. Especially now that I've decided I'm going to be a professional musician."

Jessica and Amy stared at each other, then at Lila.

"A *what*?" Amy demanded.

"You heard me." Lila brushed her hair back from her face. "You two probably think you know everything about me, but you don't. The fact is, Daddy and I have been talking about this for a while, and he thinks my becoming a musician is a really good idea. It'll help me to become more well-rounded."

Jessica stifled a grin. "This doesn't have anything to do with the fact that *you* didn't win the chance to be on Eric Parker's talk show last month, does it?"

When Eric Parker had held auditions for the coveted spot on a special edition of his talk show, both Jessica and Lila had tried out. With a lot of hard work on her part, and more than a little behind-the-scenes strategizing, Jessica had managed to convince Eric Parker that she was *much* more well-rounded than Lila. After all, Lila was the only daughter of one of the richest men in the whole state. She had been given everything in the world she ever wanted and was, at least from Jessica's perspective, more than a little spoiled. Lila's hobbies up to this point had leaned toward shopping, suntanning, and boys.

Lila Fowler a musician? It seemed a little hard to believe!

"What instrument are you planning to play?" Amy asked, concealing a smile. "The tuba?"

"Go ahead and laugh now," Lila said indifferently. "I don't care. You'll both be sorry

19

when I become a big star. You'll be begging me to introduce you to my famous friends and I won't even stop to say hello."

Jessica giggled. "When's all this going to happen, Li?"

Lila looked furious. "I happen to have a lot of musical talent. In fact, my music teacher says it's only a matter of time before we decide which instrument will be my specialty."

Amy started to giggle. "You mean, you haven't even chosen an instrument yet? How can you have a music teacher when you don't know what instrument you're going to be playing?"

"Because that's how Max Sharpe happens to work," Lila said coldly. "He's one of the best music instructors in the country. And he doesn't believe in inhibiting the natural talent of his students. We spend time together listening to different pieces, and he watches my reaction. This week I'm going over to his studio to try out some different sounds on his synthesizer. Then we're going to choose the instrument he thinks I'm best suited for."

Jessica couldn't contain her laughter anymore. "How about the xylophone?" she gasped, wiping a tear from her eye.

Amy fell back on one of the pillows, giggling

loudly. "I think you ought to make up your own instrument, Lila. Why 'inhibit your natural talent' by choosing an instrument that already exists?"

"You're both just jealous!" Lila pronounced. "Take your disc and leave. Your attitude only shows how backward you both are about *real* music."

Jessica scooped up the disc. Her giggles faded a little as she inspected the cover for the dozenth time. Even the quickest glance at Jamie Peters's image made her melt.

Lila could waste all the time she wanted pretending to study music with Max Sharpe. All Jessica wanted to do was listen to Jamie Peters's *Pride* over and over again!

On Friday evening after dinner, Todd came over to watch a movie with Elizabeth on the Wakefields' VCR. Or at least that was what they had planned to do before Jessica barged in with a bag of microwave popcorn and announced that there was a Jamie Peters special on MTV.

"We've got to watch it! He's doing an exclusive interview," Jessica cried, sitting down on the floor in front of the television and switching the channel before either Elizabeth or Todd could protest.

"Jess, we were about to watch a movie," Elizabeth complained.

"Come on, Liz. You can watch a movie anytime, but this is a chance in a million. Jamie Peters almost never does live interviews!"

Elizabeth shook her head and squeezed Todd's hand. "Sorry," she whispered. "I think our movie just got put on hold for a while."

Jessica was already glued to the screen. A young woman dressed completely in black was interviewing Jamie Peters.

"Tell us about your decision to move into films," she asked.

Jamie Peters pushed back his long blond hair, and Elizabeth exchanged a private smile with Todd. She liked Jamie Peters all right, but she thought this kind of hype was a little unnecessary.

"You know, the music business just wreaks havoc on your personal life. I hope that moving into movies will allow me a little more control over my schedule. And a little more time at home."

"I knew it!" Jessica gasped. "I bet you anything he's going to get married again. I wish they'd just come out and tell us who his girl-friend is!"

"What makes you think he's getting married again? Maybe he's just sick of being on the road," Elizabeth said.

Jessica flashed her twin an expression of utter impatience. "It's *so* obvious, Liz. You just haven't been following the whole story."

"—and besides, I *like* movies. I like new challenges, and I think it will be good for my work to try a different medium for a while," Jamie continued.

"That's what they all say," Todd remarked.

Jessica looked stricken. "What do you mean, 'they'? Jamie Peters isn't just another rock star, Todd. Don't lump him together with everybody else."

"I wasn't," Todd said mildly. "It's just—"

But Jessica had already turned back to the interview.

"We've been hearing rumors that there's a special girl in your life. Anything more you can tell us about her?" the interviewer continued.

Jessica was so intent on Jamie's answer, she looked as if she wanted to crawl inside the TV set.

"I like to keep my private life private," Jamie

answered, smiling. "But," he added softly, "she is incredibly special. I'd do anything for her."

"Wow!" Jessica breathed, her eyes wide. "Can you imagine what it must feel like being that girl?"

Elizabeth and Todd exchanged amused glances. So much for their TV date. As long as Jamie Peters was on the air, Jessica obviously was not budging!

Three

On Saturday morning, Elizabeth and Enid spread their beach towels on the sand and kept a lookout for Andrea as they smoothed on suntan lotion. It was a beautiful day. The sun was absolutely dazzling over the water and the beach was not yet crowded.

"There she is!" Enid exclaimed, pointing way down the beach to where Andrea had just appeared, laden with a big red beachbag. Both Elizabeth and Enid got up and hailed her over.

"Hi!" Andrea said as she approached. "I didn't think I'd find you guys. I don't think my beach geography is very good yet." She grinned. "I'm more used to crowded intersections than expansive beaches."

In minutes Andrea had spread out her towel and slipped out of her shorts and T-shirt. She looked ruefully at herself in her navy and white swimsuit.

"I really stand out." She sighed. "I could lie in the sun for years and never get as tanned as you are!"

"Are you kidding? In this sun, ten minutes should do the trick," Enid said.

"Yeah, you'd better use some of this." Elizabeth passed her some sunblock. "We don't want to ruin your first day at the beach with a bad sunburn!"

Andrea settled back and surveyed the scene around her with a mixture of curiosity and enthusiasm. "Beach culture." She laughed. "Tell me all about this stuff. What are those guys doing over there, for instance?"

"It's a Sweet Valley version of volleyball," Enid replied. "Volleyball and Frisbee are very popular. So is paddleball. In fact, so is anything you can play while catching some rays!"

Andrea brushed her hair back with one hand. "The most challenging sport in New York City is dodging crazy cab drivers while hanging on to your handbag so that no one swipes it. It's kind of different."

She was teasing, but Elizabeth picked up on a serious undertone in her voice.

"It must not be very easy, living in a big place like Manhattan."

Andrea was emphatic. "Oh, it was the worst! For me, anyway. Daddy and I lived in a big apartment building with about eight different elevators. You could never really tell what the weather was like. It felt as if we were factory sealed or something. We didn't have a yard, or grass or trees, and I hated my school. It was a private school and the kids were really stuck up."

"Sweet Valley must seem *so* different to you," Enid noted.

"I adore it here," Andrea declared. "I've never seen any place I like so much, and believe me, I've seen a lot of places! I've moved about ten times since I was a little kid. We've lived everywhere." She ticked off places on her fingers. "New York. Boston, before that. Dallas, Miami, Detroit—you name it! But never, ever in a place like Sweet Valley." Her eyes were bright. "I don't ever want to leave!"

Elizabeth looked at her curiously. "Why has your family moved so often?"

"My dad's business," Andrea explained. "He gets transferred a lot."

"Really?" Enid said. "What kind of business?"

Andrea shrugged. "Just—*business*."

"Your mom must hate having to move so often," Elizabeth said sympathetically.

A shadow crossed Andrea's face. "My mom died when I was really little. So it's just my father and me. But you're right, it's terrible having to move so much. I never felt that I had a real home. Especially since my father . . . well, he's fantastic, but he's kind of a workaholic."

Elizabeth was impressed by how candid Andrea was. She wasn't complaining or feeling sorry for herself, just being very honest.

"It's going to be different now, though," Andrea added. "Now that we're here."

"Will your dad have less work to do?" Enid asked her.

"Who knows?" she said. "You know fathers. They love to make promises." She paused for a minute, as if she were going to say something more. Instead she changed the subject. "Come on, you two. I'm not going to pass my class on Beach Culture unless you can explain to me what that girl is doing over there with that big piece of aluminum foil."

Enid giggled. "She's using it as a reflector, trying to get more sun on her face."

Within seconds Elizabeth, Enid, and Andrea were dissolved in laughter as they traded observations about the people around them. Elizabeth liked Andrea more than ever as she listened to her witty comments. And she seemed open and comfortable with Enid and Elizabeth, as if she genuinely liked their companionship.

Elizabeth hoped Andrea was right, that this time she and her father would be staying put!

Later that day, Elizabeth and Enid walked Andrea to the parking lot. "This is mine," Andrea said, pointing to a small white Honda. "Do either of you need a ride?"

"I drove," Elizabeth said, "but thanks, Andrea. Listen, my boyfriend Todd and a couple of his friends and Enid and I are all going to meet at the Dairi Burger tonight. Want to join us?"

"Oh, you should," Enid added when Andrea seemed to hesitate. "It's a perfect place to watch oddball behavior."

"It's got wonderful burgers, and lots of us

from school hang out there. Come on," Elizabeth urged. "It'll be fun!"

"OK. OK, sure," Andrea said, smiling. "You guys are really terrific to show me all the hot spots."

"Great!" Elizabeth continued. "Todd's picking me up at seven o'clock. Why don't we come over and get you after Enid? Or Enid, then you?" She hesitated. "Where do you live, anyway?"

"That sounds like too much trouble." Andrea paused. "How about if you just tell me where it is, and I'll meet you there," she murmured as she bent her head and rummaged through her beachbag.

"No, it's not a problem, Andrea. Todd's got a big car, and it'll be more fun to go together."

"No, really. It'll be easier for me to meet you there." Andrea pulled a pad of paper and pen out of her bag. "Just give me directions, and I'll be there at seven-thirty."

Elizabeth was about to insist again, but she reconsidered. If Andrea felt more comfortable coming on her own, she did not want to pressure her. After Enid gave her directions, Andrea hopped into her Honda, promising to meet them that evening.

"That was weird," Enid said, getting into

Elizabeth's car. "What's going on with her? You don't think that her father's involved in something illegal?"

Elizabeth laughed. "Why, just because she didn't want us to come over?"

"Well, she wouldn't even tell us where she lives," Enid pointed out. "And what's the big deal about letting us pick her up? She's new here, she shouldn't be driving around at night by herself. She could get lost."

"She seems pretty capable to me," Elizabeth commented. "Besides, maybe she's embarrassed about her home," she added. "Remember what she said yesterday, that their house was still a mess? That's probably it, Enid. Maybe they haven't unpacked anything or their house is really small. It's obvious she really cares a lot about having a home."

Enid nodded. "You're probably right. Although I think it's still kind of strange to be so secretive."

Elizabeth shrugged. She liked Andrea, but Enid was right about one thing—their new friend was definitely hiding *something*.

"Anyone home?" Elizabeth called, as she entered the kitchen.

The Wakefields' house seemed to echo. No one was in the kitchen or dining room. Through the sliding glass doors leading to the patio, she spotted Jessica sitting by the pool.

Elizabeth opened the door and went outside. Prince Albert, who had been lying beside Jessica's chair, bounded up to greet Elizabeth. Jessica, however, remained totally engrossed in reading *Rock and Roll* magazine.

"Jess, aren't you even going to say hello?" Elizabeth asked.

"Oh, hello," Jessica said, not lifting her eyes from the page.

"I don't have a sister anymore. I have a groupie." Elizabeth moaned.

Reluctantly, Jessica set the magazine down. "Did you want to say something to me?"

"Yes! I wanted to tell you about the new girl. Enid and I just spent the day at the beach with her." Elizabeth sat down on the chaise lounge closest to her sister. "Have you met Andrea Slade yet? She's from New York."

Jessica narrowed her eyes. "What does she look like?"

"Blond curly hair, pretty," Elizabeth said. "She's really tall and she has wonderful clothes. Kind of funky cotton things—very New York."

"Oh, yeah, I remember seeing her around. She does have great clothes," Jessica agreed vaguely.

"But have you met her?" Elizabeth pressed.

"Nope." Jessica looked longingly at her magazine. "Why?"

"She's a lot of fun, that's why." Elizabeth launched into a description of Andrea. "I think you'd like her a lot."

Jessica shrugged. "Lila says she's kind of weird, sort of mysterious and shy. She's probably not my type. You know you and I never like the same people, Liz. Look at Enid."

Elizabeth frowned. She hated it when Jessica criticized Enid. "Enid is the world's most loyal and sensitive girl. Compared to Amy or Lila . . ." She broke off, and Jessica laughed.

"See? My point exactly. You hang out with people like Enid, and I prefer people like Amy and Lila. But I'm sure Andrea is perfectly nice," she added, picking up her magazine again. Only Jessica could make *nice* sound like a dirty word.

"Why don't you come to the Dairi Burger with a bunch of us tonight and find out for yourself." Elizabeth offered.

Jessica yawned. "No, thanks. I'm going over to Lila's house. Her dad's on a business trip, and I think she's kind of lonely. The house-keeper goes to sleep really early, and Lila hates feeling like she's all by herself in that big house."

Elizabeth paused. "You could bring Lila, too."

"No. We're just going to hang out. You know, listen to some music, that kind of thing."

"I bet I know whose music," Elizabeth said wryly.

Jessica laughed. "I think I've practically memorized the whole first side of *Pride*. If Jamie Peters ever gives a concert here, I'll be able to sing the words to every song he plays!"

"Well, have fun. And if you change your mind, come join us at the Dairi Burger."

Elizabeth couldn't see how Jessica could possibly prefer a whole evening cooped up with Lila to a lively night with a group of friends. Well, Jessica could listen to Jamie Peters's album and drool over *Rock and Roll* magazine all she wanted. Elizabeth was much happier living in the real world. And if Jessica did not feel like being friendly to Andrea Slade, then Elizabeth certainly was not going to force her.

Four

By the middle of the next week, Andrea Slade seemed to have settled into life at Sweet Valley High. She ate lunch with Enid and Elizabeth every day, and quickly became popular with their friends.

"I really like her. She has such an original sense of humor," Olivia Davidson commented to Elizabeth one afternoon in the *Oracle* office. "I love it when she talks about New York and the other places she's lived. We ought to draft her into writing for the paper!"

Olivia was arts editor of the newspaper, and she was often on the hunt for new talent.

"Maybe we should let her settle in a little bit first. It *is* only her third week in Sweet Valley."

But Olivia would not be discouraged. She brought up the subject herself the next day at lunch. Elizabeth, Enid, Andrea, Olivia, Todd, and Winston were all sitting around the table together exchanging complaints about that day's version of "lunch."

"I can't believe they have the nerve to claim this is "all beef," Winston said, poking at the offending object with a plastic fork.

Andrea giggled. "Don't knock it, Winston. Back in New York City, that would cost you a few dollars."

Winston looked pained. "You mean they let these things cross state borders?"

Everyone giggled. Winston had been considered the unofficial clown of the junior class for some time now, and he was trying his hardest to keep up the title.

"I'm not kidding," Andrea continued. "In New York they sell these things on street corners. One time my dad . . ."

She paused, looked around for a minute, and shrugged her shoulders. "They cost a lot," she finished, somewhat weakly.

Olivia pushed her curly brown hair out of her eyes. "You should write something about the differences between New York City and Sweet Valley for the school paper, Andrea."

Andrea made a face. "I'm not a very good writer." She took a bite of her hot dog. "Besides, I'm not sure these dogs deserve to be written about. Bad lunch is bad lunch, wherever you eat it."

Olivia looked thoughtfully at Andrea. "Hey, I just remembered, my father told me that a new manager started at his firm this week. He didn't say what his name was, but I just realized that he could be *your* father. Did he move here to take a new job at Phillips Corporation?"

"Uh, no," Andrea said. Elizabeth thought she looked a little embarrassed. "He—he's actually self-employed."

"You're kidding. Is he a writer?" Olivia asked eagerly.

"No." Andrea fidgeted. "He's just . . . you know, a regular self-employed businessman." Everyone looked expectantly at her. "You know. He's an ordinary investor."

Now Winston looked interested. "Does he have an office here, or does he work at home?"

"He has an office," Andrea said slowly. She looked around the table and added, "At home, I mean."

"You know what?" Winston said, leaning forward and staring at her. "I just realized I don't even know which part of Sweet Valley you moved to."

Andrea reddened. "I don't really know how to describe it," she said faintly.

"Well, are you east or west of the marina?" Olivia asked. "Up the hill, toward Miller's Point, or more toward the middle of town, where Elizabeth and Jessica live?"

Andrea paused for a second, then shrugged. "I'm not sure. The only way I ever found my way home in New York was to ask a taxi to take me there. I've got a terrible sense of direction." She pushed her chair back and picked up her tray. "I hate to leave this party so early, but I've got to get my math homework done before class, or I'm going to be the first girl in Sweet Valley history to flunk out of school in less than three weeks."

" 'Bye, Andrea!" everyone chorused, watching her leave.

"Is she always so secretive about her father?" Winston asked once Andrea was out of earshot. "Or did I just put my foot in it—again?"

"Yeah, and what was all that stuff about not knowing where she and her father live? She can't be *that* bad with directions," Olivia chimed in.

"Why not?" Elizabeth countered. "She's only

38

been here a few weeks, and she doesn't know the area, or even this part of the country, at all. How's she supposed to know whether her house is east or west of the marina?"

"Look," Olivia said. "I like Andrea a lot. I'm not criticizing her or anything. I just wondered if she always gets so weird when you ask her about herself."

"She doesn't know any of us that well yet," Todd reminded them. "Maybe she's just a little shy."

"That's right. And it may be hard for her to talk about stuff at home. Maybe she isn't very close to her father," Elizabeth said slowly.

Privately, though, she wondered if Olivia wasn't right. Andrea seemed unusually secretive when it came to anything involving her home life.

Maybe she was just shy, as Todd had suggested. Elizabeth hoped there wasn't anything terribly wrong at home. It would be awful if someone as nice as Andrea had something so painful in her life that she couldn't share it with her friends.

"I can't wait to hear how Lila's music lessons are going," Amy said to Jessica, rolling her eyes up and giggling. It was Wednesday after school, and the girls were on their way to Lila's house to find out what instrument Max Sharpe had decided she ought to play.

It had been Lila's idea for them to come over. At lunch she had eaten a cup of frozen yogurt in five minutes flat and then jumped up to make a phone call. "I have my third lesson with Max this afternoon. Today's the day we decide what instrument I'm going to excel at," she had said blithely. "You're welcome to come over and hear the results."

"Knowing Lila, she's probably gone out and bought a baby grand piano—on her dad's credit card."

Jessica shook her head. "Well, I have to hand it to her. It takes guts to start studying an instrument at her age. Who knows? Maybe she won't be that bad."

"Maybe," Amy said. "But I don't think she has the kind of discipline you need to stick to *any* instrument."

"You're probably right. Anyway, I can't wait to see what instrument Max has chosen for her." Jessica giggled. "I hope it isn't something really loud. Can you imagine having to listen to her practice all the time?"

Lila's housekeeper, Eva, opened the door.

"Lila's upstairs," she told them. "In the music room."

"I didn't know the Fowlers had a music room," Amy whispered.

"I think it used to be a bedroom. Lila doesn't take this stuff lightly," Jessica whispered back.

Sure enough, Lila had completely transformed one of the guest rooms on the second floor of the Fowlers' mansion. Posters of classical musicians adorned the walls—Beethoven on one side, Mozart on the other, and a few rock stars in between. A music stand stood in one corner of the room, and sheet music lay in heaps on the floor. In the middle of all this, Lila was sitting perfectly still, her back straight, her hands poised and ready over something that looked to Jessica like a cross between a zither and a guitar.

"What on earth is that?" Amy cried.

Lila turned, a serene smile on her face. "Come on in. You're my very first audience. Want to hear me play the opening notes to 'Jesu, Son of Man's Desiring'?"

"Do we have a choice?" Amy muttered.

If Lila heard, she ignored Amy's remark. Her face screwed up with concentration, she leaned forward and plucked one of the metal strips that were stretched over the hole in the middle

41

of the strange wooden instrument. A thin, high note filled the room.

"What *is* that thing?" Amy demanded.

Lila plucked the second metal strip, a little higher up. "It happens to be an African instrument, Amy," she said calmly. "If you knew a little more about music, you'd recognize it. It's called a marimba. It's a distant relative of the harp," she added, pulling another strip and listening to the quavering note with satisfaction.

Jessica and Amy stared at each other and began to giggle.

"This happens to be a beautiful instrument. You're just too unsophisticated to know anything about non-Western music."

"I don't believe *this* is the instrument that Max Sharpe has chosen to highlight all your musical abilities." Amy was still gasping with laughter.

"I don't see what's so funny about it," Lila said coldly. "He says I have wonderful rhythm and a flair for the exotic. Besides, the marimba happens to be an instrument that beginners can pick up quite quickly."

Jessica wiped her eyes. "You can pick it up, all right. But can you *play* it!"

Jessica's remark made Amy break into laughter again.

Lila got to her feet, her face white. "OK. You may think this is funny, but just you wait. Once I've gotten good at this thing, you won't be laughing anymore. I guarantee it."

"Right," Jessica said. "So when you win the Miss Marimba, Sweet Valley, contest, you can tell us you told us so!"

Amy tried to squelch her hysterics. "Play some more, Lila. We'll be good, we promise."

"No way. I'm going to practice. Alone." She refused to look either Jessica or Amy in the eyes. "And when I become a big star, don't think I'm not going to remember this!"

"I think we can risk it!" Amy called behind her as they raced to the door.

Jessica couldn't remember ever laughing this hard. In fact, neither she nor Amy stopped laughing until they were halfway down the Fowlers' driveway.

Elizabeth took a sip of iced tea. "Well, I guess our tour of Sweet Valley has really gotten underway now that we've managed to get you to the mall," she said jokingly to Andrea.

It was Wednesday afternoon, and Elizabeth, Enid, and Andrea were sitting at the Garden Café on the main level of the Sweet Valley Mall, trying to work up enough energy to explore floors two and three.

"This is too much for me. I'm not used to mall culture," Andrea said, giving an exaggerated sigh. "Can't we save the second mile of stores for another day?"

Elizabeth was about to agree when a familiar voice called out her name.

"Elizabeth Wakefield! Enid Rollins!" A tall, handsome boy with dark, wavy hair waved to them from the other side of the restaurant, and Elizabeth's eyes brightened.

"It's Nicholas Morrow!" she cried, waving back and beckoning him over to join them.

Nicholas Morrow had been a friend for a long time. He was eighteen years old and was working for his father's computer company between high school and college. Until tragedy struck the Morrows, Nicholas had always seemed to be the boy who had everything. His parents were very wealthy, and they lived in one of the big estates on the hill overlooking the valley.

But in spite of his dark good looks and wonderful poise, Nicholas kept to himself a great deal, partly because he was not in high school anymore and partly because he took his job very seriously. More recently, Nicholas's time alone had had a lot to do with the death of his younger sister, Regina. Regina had been in the junior class at Sweet Valley High. She was a beautiful, talented girl who had overcome a great deal of personal difficulty, including a hearing impairment, only to die tragically of a drug overdose.

Elizabeth hadn't seen Nicholas much since Regina's death, and she was glad now for a chance to say hello.

"Hi!" she said as Nicholas came over. "Let me introduce you to a new friend. Andrea Slade, this is Nicholas Morrow. Nicholas, this is Andrea."

"Hi," Nicholas said, smiling at Andrea.

Andrea blushed and looked down at the table, without saying anything.

"What brings you to the mall on a Wednesday afternoon?" Elizabeth asked, to cover Andrea's shyness.

Nicholas held up the package in his hands. "My father needed a new software program, so I ran over here to get it from Computer Whiz." His gaze focused again on Andrea. "A new friend, huh? Are you new to Sweet Valley, or just new to Elizabeth and Enid?"

Andrea fiddled with her straw. "New completely," she said, regaining her composure a little. "I just moved here from New York."

"Wow, I know how hard *that* is," Nicholas said quickly. "My family moved here from Boston last year. It was a rough transition at first. The East Coast and West Coast are so different!"

"I lived in Boston before New York." Andrea lifted her eyes and seemed pleased to have a connection to Nicholas.

After a few minutes of conversation they discovered that Nicholas knew several of Andrea's old Boston friends. Then they spent another few minutes reminiscing about Boston.

"I loved sailing on the Charles, near the hatchshell," Nicholas said. "That was the best. You can't really get those wonderful calm days out here. And sailing is different in the ocean, anyway."

Andrea's eyes lit up. "You sail? I *love* sailing. It was one of the things I really hated about living in New York. There wasn't any way to get out on the water, except when my father took me out to Long Island."

Elizabeth nudged Enid's knee under the table. Was it her imagination, or were Andrea and Nicholas just a teeny bit interested in each other?

Nicholas appeared excited, then slightly awkward. "Well, if you like to sail, I could always

46

take you out on my boat sometime. I mean, if you'd like."

Andrea glanced at Elizabeth and Enid, and suddenly she looked as shy as she had when Nicholas had first joined them. "That would be really nice," she said quietly.

Elizabeth hid a smile. Nicholas and Andrea must really like each other, if they were having such a hard time admitting that they both wanted to take a sail together!

"I know. Tell me where you live, and I'll pick you up on Saturday on my way down to the marina." Nicholas was trying to sound nonchalant. "If you've been dying to sail all this time, we shouldn't make you wait any longer than this weekend."

Andrea's eyes were bright. "OK," she said. "But don't worry about picking me up. I've got a doctor's appointment on Saturday morning. I'll just take my car and meet you down at the marina."

"Great!" Nicholas exclaimed as he got to his feet, a big grin on his face. "It's a date."

Elizabeth felt Enid nudge her back. One thing was clear. Nicholas Morrow was the keenest new member of the Andrea Slade fan club. But not even Nicholas was going to be allowed to know where she lived!

Five

On Thursday it took Jessica and Amy several minutes to find a place to sit at lunchtime. The cafeteria was bustling with the usual noise and activity, and most of the tables were completely full.

"Over here!" Cara Walker waved to them from a table in the corner.

"This place is a madhouse," Jessica complained, setting her tray down next to Cara's.

"I've been looking for you two. What happened at Lila's? Did you get to hear the new instrument Max Sharpe chose for her?" Cara's voice was filled with curiosity. "Tell me everything!"

"Well, you missed a real treat," Amy said dryly. "Lila is going to be the most talented marimba player in Sweet Valley."

"Not to mention, the *only* marimba player," Jessica added.

"What's a marimba? It sounds like something you eat for dessert," Cara said.

Jessica giggled. "Or something to wrap your hair in."

"I think it sounds like what you yell when you're chopping down trees," Amy added with a grin. "Ma-rim-*ba*!"

Jessica began to relate the latest chapter in Lila's musical career to Cara. But before she got very far, Lila herself charged up to join them, looking as if she'd just won the lottery.

"You guys are *never* going to guess who I just saw," she gasped, sliding into her seat and wriggling out of her jacket.

"Let me see." Jessica cocked her head to one side, her forehead wrinkled in concentration. "Could it have been a famous marimba player, perhaps? Or is that a contradiction in terms?"

Lila was too excited to acknowledge Jessica's dig. "I'm serious. Listen to this! I had a dentist's appointment today at eleven-thirty, and it turned into this big crisis because I had to get special permission to miss half an hour of class, and the dentist wouldn't change the appointment. Anyway, finally my teacher let me go. So I came out of the dentist's office downtown, and who do you think I saw leaving the drugstore across the street?"

"Tell us already!" Amy said.

"Jamie Peters," Lila said smugly, sitting back and crossing her arms.

All three girls were dumbfounded. When Jessica finally found her voice, all she could get out was a choked, "No way, Lila!"

"I'm telling you, it was him. Right there in broad daylight. He had sunglasses on, but I could tell it was him in a second. I didn't know what to do. I was going to run across the street and ask him for an autograph—or just say hi—but I was in complete shock. I just kept staring at him, thinking, *this can't be him*. And by the time I realized it *was* him, he was getting into a car and driving away."

"I don't believe it," Jessica said, frowning. "You must have been imagining it, Li."

"Yeah," Amy added, with a little less conviction than Jessica. "What would Jamie Peters be doing in a drugstore in Sweet Valley?"

"What kind of Novocain does your dentist use, Lila?" Cara asked with a giggle.

"Look, think what you want to think," Lila

said dismissively. "But remember, *I'm* the one who saw him first."

Jessica was beginning to reconsider her position. "I wonder if—" she began. "Remember the article we read that said Jamie Peters was moving out to California? It's kind of hard to believe, but maybe he really *has* moved out here after all."

"Well, *I'm* the one who saw him. None of you believed me before, when I said that Jamie Peters might move to Sweet Valley." Lila put on her best wounded expression.

Amy shook her head. "I think you're all nuts. Jamie Peters is probably on location somewhere right now shooting his first movie. Somewhere like Bali or Tibet or wherever famous people go. *Not* downtown Sweet Valley."

Lila pushed her chair back in disgust. "You guys are pathetic," she said as she grabbed her jacket. "No wonder you don't appreciate a great new instrument when you hear one!"

Amy and Cara laughed, but Jessica felt a little uncomfortable. What if Lila was right? What if Jamie Peters really *had* been downtown that day?

The question was, what was he doing in Sweet Valley—and how could Jessica get to see him before anyone else did?

*   *   *

Just as Jessica had guessed, Elizabeth was completely unsympathetic when she told her that Lila thought she had spotted Jamie Peters.

"You guys have a pathological obsession. It figures you've started seeing this man now," Elizabeth said calmly, concentrating on the salad she was making for dinner. "It's the second stage of delusional behavior. Next you'll probably start hearing his music when there's no stereo or radio playing."

Jessica shook her head. "That article in *Rock and Roll* magazine said he was thinking of moving to the West Coast. You know, movie stars and rock stars *have* come to Sweet Valley before."

"You're right," Elizabeth agreed. "I suppose it could happen. But California's a big state, Jess. Wouldn't he consider Bel-Air or Malibu instead?"

Jessica sighed. She hadn't had a second's peace since Lila's frenzied announcement that day at lunch. On her way home after cheerleading practice, she had slammed on the brakes of the Fiat twice, certain she had caught a glimpse of Jamie, only to realize it was just an ordinary person.

"Listen," Elizabeth said, reaching for the salad dressing. "Enid and I want to take Andrea to the movies on Friday night, and we were wondering if you'd like to come with us. You still haven't met her."

Jessica sorted through the pile of mail on the counter. "No, thanks," she murmured. "I think Lila and Cara and Amy and I will do something."

Elizabeth frowned. "I really think you'd like Andrea, Jess. Can't you just meet us for dinner first or something?"

"I don't think so, Liz," Jessica said absently.

It wasn't that Jessica had anything in particular against Andrea Slade. It was just that right now there were so many more important things to think about. Like Jamie Peters, and whether there was even the tiniest chance that he might be in Sweet Valley at this very minute!

The Wakefields were in the middle of dinner when the telephone rang.

"I'll get it," Ned Wakefield said, a frown creasing his handsome face. One of the strict rules in the Wakefield household was that phone calls could not be taken during meals.

"I'm sorry, Lila, but Jessica is eating dinner right now," Jessica heard her father say.

Jessica stared at him, stricken. But her father hadn't hung up yet. "I see," he said slowly. "Mmm-hmm. Yes, I see. Well, if it's an emergency . . ." He covered the telephone with his hand. "Your friend Lila is calling from her car phone," he said, half amused and half annoyed. "Apparently something earth-shattering has come up, and unless she can talk to you this very second, she claims she will *die*."

Jessica looked pleadingly at her mother.

"Take it upstairs, please," Alice Wakefield said calmly. "And keep it short."

Jessica ran up to her room and slammed the door shut. "OK, Dad, I've got it," she said into the extension. She waited for the click that indicated her father had hung up before she began to talk. "Where are you?" Jessica demanded over the crackling and static on the telephone line.

Lila's voice cut through the noise. "I'm about four blocks from my house. Jess, you're not going to believe it, but I saw him again!"

"You're kidding!" Jessica felt butterflies in her stomach. This time she believed Lila. It was possible to make a mistake once and think you saw someone, but not twice—not two times in a single day! "Tell me what happened!"

"I was on my way home from Max's. I was turning left onto the road that leads toward my street when I saw the exact same car that Jamie Peters got into today downtown. It's an old white Mustang convertible. Probably vintage or something."

"What did you do? Did you follow him?" Jessica was breathless with excitement.

"Of course, I did," Lila answered as if that were the most obvious thing to do. "He went straight up the hill and took a right, and I went screeching right after him. It took all my self-control not to roll down my window and scream his name!"

Jessica twisted the telephone cord. "So what happened next?" She was extremely jealous of Lila, just then, but she didn't want Lila to notice so she kept her voice conversational.

"Well, he took that right turn, and then a second right, till he came to the drive of the old Kitterby estate. Remember that place? It's the one with the two stone posts with coral-colored stone lions."

"Yeah, I think I remember." The Kitterby place was one of the grand old estates near Lila's home.

"That estate's been for sale for months, but we never thought it would sell. Daddy said they were asking over two million for it. Whoever would've guessed in a million years that Jamie Peters—" Static and crackle cut in on Lila. "So, I'm waiting down near the entrance of the estate. I want to see if he comes out again. Maybe he's just visiting someone—"

Jessica interrupted. "I want to come right over, but I have to finish dinner first. Tell me exactly where you are, and I'll be there later," Jessica cried.

"Listen, there isn't much to see now," Lila said. "There are a few lights on in the house, and I can't see much else."

"I can't stand it! I want to come over there right now!" Jessica moaned. "It isn't fair. *I'm* the one who really likes Jamie Peters!"

"Well, just wait until you've seen him for real," Lila said smugly.

Jessica thought she was going to die. Of all the injustices. Why was Lila the one to have seen Jamie Peters first? And to have seen him twice in the same day!

It was heartbreaking.

"Listen, I've got an idea. I happen to know the Kitterby estate pretty well. When I was a kid I used to be friends with the girl who lived there. I know the layout of the gardens and pool, and I think I know a way we can sneak onto the grounds and see him up close," Lila said. "Meet me tomorrow at lunchtime, and we'll figure out a plan."

"OK." Jessica knew her parents expected her back at the table. "Are you going to stay there, or are you going home now?"

"Oh, I'll stay for a while. Just to see whether or not he comes out again."

Of all the luck! Jessica thought enviously. Well, she was just going to have to wait until she could get over to the Kitterby place and see Jamie Peters for herself. But she knew it would be agony having to wait.

The only thing that made her feel the slightest bit better was the fact that Jamie Peters was really here. Of all the places he could possibly have moved to, somehow he had chosen Sweet Valley!

Six

Andrea parked her car in one of the few free spaces left near the crowded marina on Saturday morning. She still had a few minutes before she was supposed to meet Nicholas.

She swiveled the rearview mirror down to check her appearance. Her curls, which could sometimes be on the unruly side, had been tamed with a stretchy turquoise hairband. Andrea smudged a little more of the blue eye pencil she had used to outline her eyes. She never wore eye makeup to go sailing before. But she wanted to look her best today.

Nicholas was waiting for her down at the pier. He looked even cuter this morning than she had remembered. He was wearing a pair of well-faded blue jeans, a little worn at the knees, and a white cotton polo shirt that showed off his tan.

Andrea glanced at her own pale arms. "I think I'll need a very long time on the beach before I blend in with the rest of you Californians!" she exclaimed self-consciously as she came up to Nicholas.

Nicholas smiled. "You look fine to me." He smiled, and Andrea felt herself blushing. What was it about this guy? He made her feel shy and awkward and tongue-tied—and incredibly happy—all at the same time.

"Let me tell you a little bit about my boat," he continued, walking down the pier in front of her. "It's called *Morning Glory* and it's brand new. I traded in my Sunfish for it just a few months ago." He took Andrea down to his mooring, where a beautiful sailboat bobbed in the water.

"Wow," Andrea said. "Nicholas, it's gorgeous!"

"Yeah." He looked very proud. "I wasn't sure I should go ahead with it, but I convinced myself that's one of the reasons I'm working before college." He grinned shyly. "You're the first person I'm taking out on her, though. I've been so busy lately that I've only managed to get her out a few times on my own."

"Well, that sounds like a reason to celebrate." Andrea was beginning to feel more like herself. Nicholas was so easy to be with, so friendly and open, that her shyness was wearing off quickly. Still, his smile made her stomach flip over!

"Let me get you a lifejacket. Do you feel like sailing, or would you rather be a passenger today?" he asked, jumping lightly into the boat and reaching into the cabin for the jackets.

"Why don't you do the sailing. After all, if I'm really your first passenger, I want to *act* like a passenger." Andrea stepped carefully onto the boat, feeling the welcome sway as it tipped under her weight. It had been so long since she had been sailing! Sunlight bounced off the water, and Nicholas whistled softly as he untied the mast and began to raise it. She could see he was in his element.

Ten minutes later they were ready to sail. The mast was up. Andrea untied the boat from the mooring and helped Nicholas pull up the buoy. They were off!

It took a while to catch the first breeze. "Coming about!" Nicholas cried, and Andrea deftly dodged the boom as it swung around.

The white sails snapped out straight in the breeze, and the beautiful little boat jumped forward. Andrea sat up straight, loving the way the wind felt in her hair.

"Is this OK?" Nicholas called as the boat began to heel.

"Great!" she called back over the wind.

For the next fifteen or twenty minutes, they sailed toward the edge of the bay. It was impossible to make conversation sailing at this speed, but Andrea was in heaven. She could not remember the last time she had been this happy. The sun was hot on her bare arms and legs, but the spray of ocean water cooled her. Everything around her was a dazzle of colors: blue sea, bright white sails. Nicholas's dark hair rippled in the wind, and every once in a while he glanced back from the bow and gave her a thumbs-up sign.

"Listen, the wind's dying down a little," he called after a while. "How about we just drift?"

"That sounds great." Andrea moved forward to join him in the front of the boat. "Nicholas, this is incredible."

His eyes were bright. "Isn't it? I love coming out here. It makes me feel . . . I don't know how to put it. I guess it's a mixture of peaceful and excited."

"Yeah, I know exactly what you mean."

Nicholas pulled himself up so he was sitting right next to her. "You know, this is pretty special for me," he said softly. "I didn't think—I don't know, I'm not sure I really imagined bringing anyone out here with me for a long time."

Andrea looked at him uncertainly. His expression had suddenly turned very grave.

"My younger sister died a few months ago," he said, swallowing hard. "I don't know why I'm telling you this, except, well, I guess I'd like us to get to know each other. And Regina's death—well, it's the biggest thing for me right now. I guess when I bought this boat, I felt like I was doing it for her, in a weird way." He looked out at the water. "Regina really loved sailing."

Andrea bit her lip. She was surprised that Nicholas was confiding in her on their first date. She felt very flattered that he trusted her this way.

"Listen, I don't even know anything about you," Nicholas said suddenly, and trying, with effort, to change the subject. "Except that you've lived all over the country and you like to sail." He leaned forward, his hand lightly touching her hair. "And you have beautiful curls," he added softly.

Andrea blushed and pulled back. "I—I'm just your average high school girl," she murmured. She felt awkward under his intense scrutiny. It would be so wonderful to confide in Nicholas, to tell him everything! She really liked him. Maybe she could trust him, too.

But I made myself a promise, Andrea thought stubbornly. *This time is going to be different. People are going to like me for me, and that's all there is to it!*

"OK," Nicholas said, settling back and putting his hands under his head. "If you're going to make this hard, Miss Slade, I'll just have to grill you." He grinned. "What's your favorite color?"

"Blue," she said promptly.

"Favorite food?" he continued.

"Umm, pasta, I think. There's this one kind—" Andrea blushed a little, feeling silly but also enjoying this way of revealing things about herself. "It's called angel hair. I had it once with cream sauce and fresh herbs."

They kept this game up for a long time, trading favorites—favorite sports, favorite movies, favorite countries. Favorite places to be alone. Andrea was amazed by how much they had in common. They both liked baseball, Italian restaurants, reggae music, and anyplace warm. They both agreed that the best place to be alone would be near the ocean, if possible. "This would do," Andrea said, jerking her chin in the direction of the pier. Nicholas nodded his agreement.

"Now, for unfavorites," Andrea said and grinned. "Gym class is up there."

"Monday mornings," Nicholas said grimacing.

"Moving vans."

Nicholas looked at her more closely. "You've moved a lot, huh?"

Andrea shrugged, sensing danger. This was the kind of question that could easily turn into another tell-me-more-about-yourself command.

"Muzak in elevators," she added quickly, before he could ask anything more.

Nicholas let his hand slip down so it was covering hers. "You're making me nervous. What if it turns out you happen to consider boys named Nicholas unfavorites? Then where would I be?"

"Silly," Andrea said, dropping her eyes. She tried to pull her hand back, but Nicholas was too quick for her. He held tight, and his fingers were warm over hers. Andrea felt her heart begin to beat a little bit faster.

"For instance, suppose I just happened to have a thing about girls named Andrea?" he said softly, leaning closer so she felt his breath against her ear.

Andrea's heart pounded. If she moved just a tiny little bit, she knew he would kiss her.

"Nicholas, wait. I'm just not—" She jerked back, completely confused, and pulled her hand free from his. Nicholas seemed surprised and a little hurt. But he didn't say anything as he moved to the stern.

"Actually," Andrea said, as he began to turn the boat around toward shore, "Nicholas happens to be my favorite boy's name."

Nicholas was the one who suggested going out for dinner that night. Andrea had a feeling she really shouldn't. She wasn't ready to tell Nicholas her secret. But she was having such a great time she just couldn't say no.

"Let's see. We need a place that has very special pasta, right? Angel hair with fresh herbs and cream sauce," Nicholas said teasingly.

Andrea nodded. "Right. And a boy named Nicholas." She was amazed at how forward she sounded. But Nicholas made her feel so confident and self-assured.

"Great! I think I know just the place to take you," Nicholas said. "I'll pick you up at seven."

Andrea hesitated. If Nicholas saw her home, her secret would be out in the open. But it would seem very strange to meet him at the restaurant. "Nicholas," she said slowly, "our house is still a complete mess. I think it would be a lot easier if I came over to your house, and we went from there."

Nicholas bent over the boat and secured the rope. When he stood up again, he looked really hurt.

"It isn't me, is it?" he asked seriously.

"Of course not!" Andrea cried. "It's just— you know how crazy things can be after a move," she said, somewhat feebly.

"Maybe after a while I can pick you up at your house," he murmured. "Unless you're ashamed of me for some reason."

Andrea felt stung. She hadn't meant to offend Nicholas. It was the last thing she had wanted to do.

But she could not think of anything to tell him, except the truth. And she was not ready to do that. She really liked Nicholas, and she wanted him to like *her*, Andrea Slade.

Once he came to her house, she was afraid that wouldn't be possible anymore. It would be like all the other times. And Andrea just could not bear to let that happen again.

"OK, I have to admit it. You've found what must be the only restaurant in Southern California that specializes in angel hair pasta," Andrea joked.

It was eight o'clock, and she and Nicholas were sitting in the garden courtyard of Oggi, an Italian restaurant on the outskirts of Sweet Valley. It was a lovely restaurant. Tiny lights hanging in the trees above them created a romantic aura. Despite her efforts to keep the conversation between them light, Andrea could tell that the romance of the place was having an effect on them both.

"I don't want to say anything I shouldn't," Nicholas said after they had ordered their dinners. "But I was hoping . . ." He looked straight at her. "I'm a pretty direct person, and when I feel something, I usually just come right out and say it. Andrea, I like you. A lot."

Andrea felt butterflies in her stomach. "I like you too, Nicholas," she said softly.

He cleared his throat. "Do you think I could see you again? After tonight, I mean?"

Andrea laughed. "Of course," she said happily.

A smile of relief broke over Nicholas's face, and Andrea knew her own expression was equally delighted. *He likes me, for myself,* she thought, still hardly daring to believe it.

For Andrea, most of the evening passed in an enchanted blur. She and Nicholas traded stories. He told her a little about Regina and his family, and she told him about some of her experiences in New York and Boston.

"Just promise me you won't move away from Sweet Valley anytime soon," Nicholas said at one point, taking her hand.

Andrea did not know what to say. She had been thinking the very same thing. But what she couldn't tell Nicholas was that it was not up to her.

How could she convince her father that they *had* to stay in Sweet Valley? Could she possibly make him understand how important it was for her to stay here—here, where she could be just a girl like any other girl her own age?

"I'll try to stick around," she said lightly.

She could hardly believe it when Nicholas told her it was eleven-thirty. "Time to take you home, Cinderella. Or your car's going to turn into a pumpkin—right out there in front of my house!"

Andrea smiled. "This was a wonderful evening, Nicholas." She shook her head. "I hope you're not trying to spoil me."

"Well, if that's what you're afraid of, let me take you to the Dairi Burger tomorrow night. You won't think I'm spoiling you then!"

Andrea laughed. "You've got a deal. How about I meet you there at about seven o'clock?"

A shadow crossed Nicholas's face, but he said nothing. Not until they had reached his house. Holding Andrea's hand tightly in his, Nicholas walked her to her car.

"One of these days you're going to let me pick you up and take you home," he said softly. "Like a real date."

"One of these days," Andrea murmured. She was glad he couldn't see her face. She was afraid her expression might give something away.

"Andrea." He tipped her face up and looked searchingly in her eyes.

"Thanks for a fantastic day," she began, struggling to keep her composure.

But she lost the struggle. Nicholas took her in his arms and kissed her, and Andrea forgot everything but how wonderful it felt to be held by him. She did not want the moment to stop, ever. And she really meant it when she told him she couldn't wait to see him again the next evening.

Seven

Jessica was practically going out of her mind with impatience by the time she reached Lila's house on Saturday morning. "This has been the longest day and a half of my whole life," she blurted out when Lila came to the door.

For once, Lila resisted the temptation to act smug. "I know," she commiserated, closing the door behind them with a sigh. "Believe me, don't you think I've wanted to drive past the Kitterby place a hundred times since Thursday? But it isn't worth getting caught snooping. We've got to do this right."

"I guess so," Jessica said unhappily, following Lila into the living room. "But yesterday after school . . ."

"I had my marimba lesson," Lila reminded her.

Jessica bit her lip. She controlled her impulse to make a biting comment about Lila's marimba. She could not risk getting Lila mad at her now. Lila was the only one who knew the secret spying place at the Kitterby mansion, and until she had shown her, Jessica knew she had better stay on her friend's good side.

"Where's Amy? She's late," Jessica grumbled. They were supposed to meet at Lila's house at eleven, and it was already almost eleven-thirty.

Before Lila could answer, the door bell rang, and a moment later, Amy rushed in, her eyes big with excitement.

"I can't believe this!" she crowed. "I can't believe that Jamie Peters is really living in Sweet Valley!"

Lila looked extremely proud of herself. "I knew it," she said smugly. "I was the one who thought he might move here. And I was the one who saw him first," she reminded Amy.

Amy didn't like her tone of voice. "Big deal, Li. You don't own him just because you happened to be the first to see him!"

Lila crossed her arms. "You weren't so interested in him before. Now, just because he happens to be living here—"

Jessica could sense trouble brewing. "Look, what's the point of arguing?" she said reasonably. "I don't know about you two, but I'd much rather go over to the Kitterby place and check this out for myself. *If* Jamie Peters is really living there."

"He really is," Lila cut in, even more upset now. "Do you still think I'm just making the whole thing up?"

"Come on!" Jessica pleaded. "Let's go already, Lila."

"Well, all right," Lila said, partly mollified. "But we have to be perfectly quiet. I'll tell you how the Kitterby place is laid out first, because once we're on the grounds we can't so much as whisper."

"Don't you think Lila's taking this just a little too seriously?" Amy asked when Lila disappeared into the kitchen, looking for paper and a pencil with which to draw a map.

"Maybe the marimba lessons are getting to her," Jessica answered with a shrug.

But there was nothing they could do but feign interest while Lila showed them the exact layout of the Kitterby estate in grueling detail.

"See?" she said, drawing a big oblong. "This

is the swimming pool, which is behind the house. There's a Mexican-tile patio around the pool, and behind that a bunch of thick bushes. Calla lily, I think," Lila said, chewing thoughtfully on her pencil.

"Lila, please," Jessica begged. "Just get on with it."

"OK, OK. Anyway, behind the trees and bushes there's this long trail, which leads out into the parkland behind their house. All we have to do is walk up to the park, pick up the trail, and take it back to the Kitterby place."

"And once we're there, what do we do?" Amy demanded.

"The bushes are thick enough to hide us. If we crouch behind them, we should be able to have a pretty good view. I know because Alexis Kitterby and I used to play hide-and-seek there," Lila said. "So we just hide behind the bushes and wait for Jamie Peters to come out to the pool."

"Great! What are we waiting for, then?" Amy cried.

Lila got to her feet, a warning look on her face. "Just remember to keep *absolutely* quiet. If Jamie Peters hears something and calls the police, we're in real trouble."

"Does that mean you aren't going to bring your marimba?" Amy asked and giggled.

Lila ignored Amy's remark. "Come on," Lila said, her head held high.

On the way over to the Kitterby place, she added, as if in response to Amy's jibe, "You know, now that another serious musician has moved into the neighborhood, I think I'm going to arrange for him to hear me play."

"Play?" Amy exclaimed, staring at her unbelievingly.

"Yes," Lila said calmly. "Why not? Jamie Peters has a wonderful ear for authentic, interesting instruments. He'll probably be overjoyed that there's a marimba player living five houses away from him."

"You don't mean . . . you wouldn't *play* that thing in public, in front of Jamie Peters," Amy faltered, absolutely horrified.

Lila raised her eyebrows. "Wait and see."

Amy was about to say something more, but Lila put her fingers to her lips. "We're at the entrance of the path now. Not another word," she whispered.

Fifteen minutes had gone by since the three girls crouched down behind the calla lily bushes bordering the large pool at the Kitterby estate. So far, they had seen absolutely nothing.

"My knees hurt," Amy complained in a loud stage whisper.

"Shh!"

Jessica sympathized with Amy. *Her* knees hurt, too. The shrubs grew quite densely, and there wasn't enough room to stretch. Each of the girls wanted the perfect peephole in case Jamie Peters happened to come outside, and that meant crouching, eyes straining ahead through the thick shrubs.

"Yikes! There's a bee in here." Amy shifted sideways and swatted wildly at the air.

"Cut it out!" Lila chided her.

"Lila, I don't think anyone's even home," Jessica whispered. The Kitterby estate was a beautiful Spanish-style villa, a sprawling stucco house with red tiles on the roof. The back doors were sliding glass, so the girls could see through to the living room. But there seemed to be no one inside. And outside, the aqua-blue pool was completely still. A few deck chairs lay scattered around, but the only sign that someone might be home was a pair of sunglasses on the table. Otherwise, the place seemed deserted.

"Just give it time. You two would make lousy spies," Lila said.

Amy stopped shooing the bee and concentrated on trying to flex her leg muscles. "I have a cramp now," she said.

"Try sitting down and wiggling your foot," Jessica whispered.

She was about to give Amy a little more room when she heard something.

"That's him! Look!" Lila gasped, grabbing Jessica's arm.

All three girls squinted through the shrubs. Jessica could feel her heart begin to pound. Sure enough, the glass door slid open—and out stepped Jamie Peters.

Jessica thought she was going to faint. She felt as if she knew Jamie Peters by heart. She had studied his face so many times on posters, on TV, in *Rock and Roll* magazine. And now here he was, in flesh and blood, standing less than a dozen yards away!

He was even more handsome in real life than Jessica could possibly have imagined. He was tall, for one thing, and well built. She could see that from what he was wearing—a pair of faded blue jeans and a white cotton shirt, unbuttoned just enough to show off a gorgeous tanned chest.

Jessica blinked. "I don't believe this," she whispered, clutching Lila's arm. "Pinch me. Tell me this is really happening."

Lila stared straight ahead, rapt. Even Amy was dumbstruck. Jamie ambled slowly to the table where the glasses were lying, picked them up, and squinted lazily at the sky. He was holding a portable phone in his other hand. After a couple of minutes he dropped the sunglasses and punched seven numbers on the phone.

"Leo? It's Jay," he said.

Hearing his voice almost undid Jessica. There it was, that sultry, low, confident voice she knew so well from TV interviews.

"I need to talk to you about that Grierson deal," he said. All three girls were hanging on his every word. "No, that's partly the point. She isn't here right now."

She? Was he talking about his girlfriend—the "special girl" he wrote all those wonderful songs for?

"Well, check it out and let me know. But remember, it's a surprise," Jamie continued.

"This is unreal!" Amy hissed.

"Shh!" Lila hissed back.

Jamie turned in their direction, a slightly confused expression on his face.

Lila's eyes registered panic. "Follow me," she

ordered under her breath. And before Amy or Jessica could protest, she was off like a shot.

"I don't see why you had to run off," Amy gasped when they had reached the top of the path in the parkland. Like Lila, she was red-faced and out of breath from excitement and the exertion.

"He heard us! He could've stepped into the bushes in a second and found us!"

"I could've stayed there forever," Amy said dreamily. "Wow, imagine what everyone at school will say when we tell them!"

"They're *not* going to know," Lila said fiercely.

"What do you mean?"

"Just what I said. If anyone else finds out about this, it'll be all over school. We won't be able to keep Jamie Peters to ourselves."

Jessica nodded. "Lila's right, Amy. We shouldn't tell anyone."

"Not even Cara?" Amy asked.

"OK, Cara," Lila conceded. "But that's it. Nobody else."

For once, Jessica agreed completely with Lila. Seeing Jamie Peters so close—in his very own home—was one of the most magical things that had ever happened to her. And right now, she didn't want anyone else in on their special secret.

Andrea pulled into the parking lot of the Dairi Burger just after Nicholas on Sunday night.

"Hi!" Nicholas walked over to her car, a big smile on his face.

"Hi, yourself." Andrea couldn't believe how good it was to see him again. This was a new feeling for her. Was this what it was like, having a crush on a boy?

"I tried to make reservations," Nicholas joked, nodding his head toward the brightly lit hamburger joint, "but they said we would have to just take our chances."

As usual, Andrea's shyness vanished as soon as he spoke. She followed Nicholas into the restaurant, once again struck by how easy it felt to be with him. Easy and exciting both, she corrected herself.

"Now, they don't serve angel hair pasta here," Nicholas said once they were seated in a corner booth.

Andrea pretended to be upset. "How can you do this to me? And I had my heart set on it."

His fingers inched over toward hers. "How come it feels so good to see you again?" His voice was raspy, and Andrea felt her cheeks turn pink.

"I don't know," she whispered, her eyes on his. "But I know it feels pretty great to see you, too."

The cheerful din around them seemed to evaporate. Andrea was aware only of Nicholas's smile and the warmth of his hands on hers.

Something told her this was not just a casual flirtation or a crush. Something real seemed to be starting up between them, and for once, Andrea did not want to question it or put her emotions in check.

This is what it's like to be an ordinary, happy teenage girl, she told herself. No matter what, she was not going to give up that sensation.

Whatever it took, this was the world Andrea wanted. And now that she had it, she never wanted to leave it behind!

Eight

"I don't believe it!" Cara gasped. It was lunch hour on Monday, and Jessica, Amy, and Lila had just finished telling her about their adventure at Jamie Peters's house.

"Well, you'd better believe it, because it's true," Amy said happily. "And don't tell a single soul, either. The four of us are the only ones who know!"

"Remember how I said I thought he'd move here to Sweet Valley?" Lila reminded everyone for the tenth time. "I swear, I must be omniscient or something."

"And you actually *saw* him?" Cara continued, her eyes wide with amazement.

"Clear as day. He was just a few yards away from us. We could even hear the conversation he was having on his cordless phone," Jessica informed her.

"I want to see him," Cara said quickly. "When do I get to go over to the Kitterby place with you and see Jamie Peters for myself?"

Lila looked at Jessica and Amy. "I don't know," she said slowly. "I'm supposed to have a lesson with Max this afternoon."

"Oh, by the way, Lila, I saw an article in the newspaper this weekend on that instrument you're learning to play," Cara told her. "What's it called again?"

"The marimba," Lila said proudly.

"Yeah, that's it. The article said that it's one of the hottest new instruments among young musicians."

"See? I told you guys! Just wait till I get an audition with Jamie Peters! He'll help me become famous overnight."

Cara looked flabbergasted. "You're going to play in front of a famous rock star? But you've only been taking lessons for a couple of days!"

"I happen to have natural talent for the marimba. That's what Max Sharpe thinks. Besides, I'm not crazy. I'm not going to play for

Jamie until I'm much better. At least not for another week or two!"

"Lucky Jamie," Jessica said sarcastically. "He's going to be *so* glad he picked Sweet Valley over Hollywood."

"I'm dying to see Jamie Peters for myself." Cara cut in. "Lila, if you've got a lesson, maybe Jessica and Amy can take me."

"No!' Lila cried. "I mean, I'd better come with you," she added hastily, embarrassed by her outburst. "It's just—you know, it's tricky finding the right way in, and someone has to be there to keep Jessica and Amy quiet. On Saturday they practically gave us away."

"Lila doesn't want us going over there without her. She seems to think she has some kind of patent on Jamie Peters these days," Amy grumbled.

Lila ignored this. "We'll go back, but on one condition. No one can make a single peep. No whispering, and no complaining about bees!" She turned apologetically to Cara. "I know *you* won't be this way, but Jessica and Amy just couldn't control themselves."

"I promise to be quiet. I just want to see him for myself, that's all."

"All right," Lila said sternly. "But I'm serious about this. If you guys blow it and make noise,

I'm going to call Jamie Peters on the telephone and tell him you were spying on him!"

On the other side of the lunchroom, Elizabeth, Enid, Olivia, and Dana Larson were having lunch with Andrea. Elizabeth couldn't get over how beautiful Andrea looked.

"What's different about you? Did you do something to your hair?" she asked.

Andrea shook her head. "I'm catching a cold, that's the only thing different," she said, reaching for a tissue.

"Somehow I don't think that's it." Elizabeth turned to Enid. "Doesn't she look different?"

"I think *I* know," Enid said dramatically. "I happen to have heard from two reliable sources that you and Nicholas Morrow had dinner at the Dairi Burger last night."

"You did?" Andrea blushed.

"Well?" Enid prompted. "Did you?"

Andrea laughed. "Yes, Nicholas and I had dinner together. Not only last night, but Saturday night, too."

"Wow," Olivia Davidson said, reaching for a french fry. "That's pretty big stuff, Andrea. Nicholas is fantastic. I'm really glad for you."

"Whoa!" Andrea exclaimed, putting up her

hand. "What are you glad about? It's no big deal having dinner with a friend, is it?"

"Yeah, but two dinners," Dana pointed out, "are different from one. And Nicholas Morrow is way too hunky to be just a friend."

Andrea blushed again.

"Not to mention the fact that you're blushing," Olivia added cheerfully.

"OK, I admit it. I think Nicholas is pretty nice." Andrea glanced around the table anxiously. "There isn't anything I should know about him that I don't know already, is there? Like, he doesn't have a girlfriend somewhere, does he?"

"Nope," Dana assured her. "He comes from a really wealthy family, but you can probably deal with that."

This time Andrea reddened in earnest. "Oh."

Elizabeth caught Enid's eye. If it was true that Andrea was ashamed of her home, for whatever reason, it probably had not helped to learn that Nicholas was so well off.

"Nicholas is a wonderful guy," Elizabeth said warmly, hoping Andrea would not get the wrong impression from the others. "He's smart, sensitive—he's really great."

"Yeah, all that stuff he's gone through since

Regina died. Did he tell you about that?" Dana asked.

"A little bit." Andrea nodded. "It sounded horrible."

"It *was* horrible," Enid agreed. "I think a lot of us are still trying to get over it. And I don't know how his family is coping. His parents have been absolutely devastated. They blame themselves. They still feel that if they'd been more protective of her, her death could have been avoided."

Everyone was quiet for a minute. Finally, Andrea cleared her throat. "Well, I'm glad he was able to trust me enough to tell me about it," she said softly.

Elizabeth watched Andrea closely as Olivia and Dana changed the subject to something less painful. She had a distinct sense that Andrea really cared about Nicholas, and Elizabeth thought they would make a great couple.

She couldn't help wondering, though, if Andrea was as secretive about her home life with Nicholas as she had been with Enid and Elizabeth.

Somehow Elizabeth doubted it. It was one thing to hold off a little bit with friends. But if Andrea and Nicholas were getting romantically involved—and it sure seemed as if they were!—

Andrea wouldn't be able to keep very much a secret from him. At least, not for long.

"If I'd known we were going to have to listen to a marimba concert, I'm not sure I would've even come this afternoon," Amy muttered.

"Shhh," Jessica warned her. Jessica, Amy, and Cara were lined up patiently at one end of Lila's newly converted "music room," waiting for Lila to master the song she had insisted on playing for them before they headed over to the old Kitterby place.

"I'm ready." Lila sat up straight over the marimba. She plucked experimentally at one metal strip, and it emitted a now-familiar sound. Several individual plucks followed, succeeded by a rapid-fire arpeggio.

"Wow," Cara said, impressed by her friend's performance. "You've really learned fast."

"What *was* that?"

"It's an African tune, Amy. You wouldn't know it," Lila said dismissively.

"It's kind of pretty, in a weird way," Jessica admitted.

"Weird, yes. Pretty, I'm not so sure about." Amy crossed her arms over her chest.

"Listen, Li, I think it's great that you're learning an instrument. It takes a lot of guts to try something new," Cara said generously.

Lila sat back, a self-satisfied smile on her face. "If Eric Parker could hear me now, I don't think there's any question about who would've won the spot on his talk show."

Jessica felt like taking back her earlier compliment. Nothing infuriated her more than Lila's way of bringing up that competition and suggesting that *she* should have won instead of Jessica.

But Cara intervened. "This is probably the right time to head over to the Kitterby place," Cara said swiftly.

Lila wasn't finished yet, though. "Max says I'm almost ready to give my first concert."

Jessica groaned. "You've got to be kidding! How can you expect people to listen to you on that thing?"

"Jessica Wakefield, you don't know the first thing about music!"

"Come on, you two," Cara pleaded weakly.

"Yeah, let's not sit around here arguing. If we're going to see Jamie, I want to leave right now," Amy seconded.

"OK," Lila said grumpily. "Then let's go already."

On the walk over to the Kitterby estate, Lila,

Amy, and Jessica reminded Cara of what had happened on Saturday. "It's kind of crowded behind those bushes. We might want to take turns this time, because there are four of us."

"We just *have* to be quiet," Lila repeated urgently. "I can just see the look on my dad's face if Jamie Peters catches me spying on him. I'd be in such big trouble."

Jessica couldn't resist an extra little dig. "You should've brought your marimba, Lila," she hissed as they neared the top of the path into the estate. "Why not just serenade Jamie from the bushes?"

Lila gave her a murderous look, but they were too close to the Peters estate for her to respond as loudly as she would have liked.

"Cara, you go first," Lila whispered, pointing the way toward the clearing behind the calla lily bushes.

Cara walked ahead, followed by Amy, Lila, and Jessica. Soon all four were bunched up behind the bushes, peering at the closed glass door.

This time they did not have to wait as long to catch a glimpse of their idol. Jamie Peters came outside only minutes later. From the way he was dressed—a bathing suit and towel—it appeared as if he had been outside all afternoon and just gone in for a minute, maybe to replenish the drink in his hand.

"Wow!" Cara breathed, enraptured.

Lila held her finger warningly to her lips, and Cara nodded. Jessica could see from the excitement in Cara's eyes what an effect it had on her to see the rock star up close.

For Jessica, it wasn't quite as much of a thrill this time. Oh, it was wonderful seeing Jamie Peters all right. But she felt a little impatient, crouching there in utter silence and just *watching* him. Her mind began to race. Suppose someone happened to make a noise—maybe Jessica herself. Jamie would come racing over to see what was wrong. He would be worried, of course. The others would probably run off, too scared to stay. Jamie would be tender and kind. He might offer her a soda or an iced tea. They would get to talking, and before long . . .

"Hey," Lila whispered, her eyes wide. She poked Jessica in the ribs and pointed toward the glass door, which was opening again.

"I've been looking everywhere for you!" a feminine voice called.

All four girls peered eagerly through the shrubbery for a better view. At first, Jessica couldn't see much. It was a woman—a young woman. No, a girl. She had her hair pulled back and sunglasses on, and a white towel was wrapped around what looked like a black bathing suit.

"His girlfriend!" Lila breathed.

The girl padded around the side of the pool and gave Jamie a tender kiss on the cheek. She let her blond curls loose with one hand and with the other, slid off her sunglasses. She looked almost directly at the spot where the girls were crouching.

No one said a word. Jessica could hear her heat pounding wildly. She took a deep breath and, willing herself to be soundless, inched away from the bushes. Lila, Cara, and Amy followed. When they reached the top of the path, they broke into a run and didn't stop until they were out of earshot.

"I don't believe it!" Amy gasped.

"What on earth is *he* doing with *her*!" Lila cried.

"She's way too young for him!" Cara exclaimed.

"I guess that's a big star for you," Jessica said bitterly. "He could have anyone in the world! Why would he go for her?"

The shock and amazement were too much for any of them. Jessica felt her face burn as she went over the scene in her mind's eye.

The last person in the world she ever would have expected to be Jamie Peters's "special girl" was Andrea Slade.

But that was exactly who the girl at the pool had been. And what other explanation could there be for her appearance there?

"I've heard she's kind of secretive about her home life," Cara mused.

"Well, now we know why," Lila said with satisfaction. "Who wouldn't want to keep it a secret? Andrea Slade is probably the only high school junior we know who's the live-in girl-friend of a world-famous rock star!"

Nine

Elizabeth got to school early on Tuesday morning. She had to go over the copy for "Eyes and Ears," the gossip column she wrote for the newspaper.

Olivia was already in the newspaper office when Elizabeth arrived.

"You, too?" Olivia asked with a look of mock anguish. "Why aren't there just two more days in every week? Then we could get all this stuff finished on time!"

"Three more," Elizabeth corrected her. She sat down at her desk and reached for the copy. "Hey, this is strange," she said, tearing off a piece of looseleaf paper that had been pinned to the packet of copy. "What's this? I thought I already had all the entries for the column."

"Oh, I found that in our mailbox when I came in this morning. Someone must've dropped it off after classes yesterday. Unless there's a maniac who gets to school even earlier than I do."

Elizabeth unfolded the piece of paper. "To the editor of 'Eyes and Ears,' " she read aloud. "You'd better add this to your column this week." At the bottom of the page was scrawled: "Time to ask Andrea Slade about her relationship to the famous rock star we happen to know has just moved to Sweet Valley."

Elizabeth frowned. "I don't get it." She handed it to Olivia. "Can you figure out what this means?"

"No. It's probably just a hoax," she said and shrugged.

Just then the office door opened and Penny Ayala burst in. Penny, a tall brunette with lots of energy, was editor in chief of *The Oracle*. This morning it appeared that she had a major news flash on her hands. "You guys will never believe this. Guess who moved into the old Kitterby estate up on the hill?"

Elizabeth and Olivia looked at her expectantly.

"Jamie Peters!" Penny could barely contain

her excitement. "No one's supposed to know about it yet, but I've got a friend who works on the entertainment page of *The Sweet Valley News*, and apparently the secret's out. Some real estate agent blabbed it to the press, and by tonight it'll be on every news channel."

Elizabeth stared down at the piece of paper in her hand. "Wow!" she said. "The old Kitterby place. Did your friend happen to say when Jamie moved here?"

Penny shook her head. "I don't think so. A few weeks ago, maybe. It's a miracle he kept it a secret this long, don't you think?"

Elizabeth's mind was buzzing. Andrea had been so secretive about her father. All she had said was that he often transferred and that he was "self-employed." It was a long shot, but was it possible that Andrea's father was Jamie Peters?

"Where's Andrea? Have you seen her today?" Elizabeth asked Enid the minute they met in the lunch line that day.

"She's home sick with a bad cold," Enid told her. "She called me this morning and asked if I'd take notes for her in social studies. Why?"

"Oh." Elizabeth shrugged. Why not tell

96

Enid? The rumors were already buzzing around school, so it wasn't as if she were telling her friend something she wouldn't hear any minute from someone else. "Have you heard that Jamie Peters has moved to Sweet Valley?"

"No way!" Enid stared at Elizabeth, her eyes widening. "Here? To Sweet Valley? You've got to be kidding!"

"No, it's true. Penny Ayala told me this morning. He bought that big old Spanish villa up near Nicholas and Lila." Elizabeth helped herself to a salad as they moved through the line.

"And what does that have to do with Andrea?" Enid asked, puzzled.

"Look at this." Elizabeth handed Enid the folded sheet of looseleaf she had received that morning.

"Wow." Enid scanned the message rapidly. She was quiet for a minute, apparently trying to soak in the news. "I don't get it. Is Jamie . . ." She paused. "He isn't her *father*, is he?"

"It's possible. It would explain a lot, too. Why they have to move so often. And why Andrea's been so secretive about what he does for a living."

"I wish Andrea were here today. I'd love to come right out and ask her," Enid said. " 'Cause to tell you the truth, I still don't get it. Even if he is her father, why not tell us? She trusts us, doesn't she?"

Elizabeth couldn't answer that one. It was something she had been wondering herself.

No sooner had they headed toward the tables than Elizabeth and Enid were bombarded. Jessica and Lila bore down on them from one side, and what seemed like a mob of girls came down on the other—Amy, Cara, and Caroline Pearce.

"Where's Andrea?" Lila asked eagerly. "Have you two seen her today?"

"Yeah, she's always with you," Jessica added.

"She happens to be home sick," Enid answered.

"Sick. I bet," Lila said knowingly.

Elizabeth and Enid were confused. "What do you mean by that?" Enid asked.

"You mean, you two don't even know? I thought you were such good friends with her." Lila grinned. "Of course Andrea would rather stay at home than come to school. Andrea Slade is Jamie's live-in girlfriend!"

Elizabeth felt the color drain from her face. "How can you possibly say a thing like that?" she choked out.

"You'd better watch it," Enid said in a low voice. "That's a pretty rotten accusation to make. And how do *you* know anything about Andrea Slade's private life?"

"We have our ways," Amy said smugly.

Elizabeth and Enid set their trays down, and the rest of the girls surrounded them, pulling up chairs and talking excitedly about Andrea and Jamie Peters.

"I wonder how long they've been together. Do you think she was a groupie or something?" Caroline asked, her eyes shining with curiosity.

"Silly, that stuff only happens in tabloids. I bet they met somewhere wonderful, some glitzy hot spot in New York." Amy propped her chin on her hand and she smiled dreamily.

"I'd like to know what you guys are basing these rumors on." Elizabeth suddenly felt unable to eat a single bite of her lunch.

"Let's just say we happened to see the two of them together. At home." Lila's smug expression seemed to deepen by the minute.

"Great. So you mean you were spying," Elizabeth snapped.

"Who said anything about spying? We were just . . . paying close attention," Amy said with a giggle.

Elizabeth glared around the table. "Well, I

don't care what you guys saw, or thought you saw. Just because Andrea happened to be with Jamie Peters doesn't mean she's his girlfriend. Did you ever stop to consider that he could be her *father?*"

Her outburst seemed to stun the girls. It was clear that none of them had even considered the possibility that Andrea was Jamie Peters's daughter.

But they weren't prepared to take it very seriously—at least, not for long.

"Right," Amy said sarcastically. "Tell me Jamie Peters is old enough to be Andrea's father!"

"Maybe he's her older brother, then," Enid suggested.

"I don't see why you two are so resistant to the truth. What's wrong with having a friend who's got great connections?" Lila asked. "Actually, I wouldn't mind getting to be better friends with Andrea myself."

"Me neither," Jessica added. "I'm sorry I didn't get to know her better before."

"I'm going to invite her over to my house the second she gets back to school," Amy chimed in.

"You're awful, all of you!" Elizabeth was madder than she had been in a long time.

"Andrea's going to know you're not genuinely interested in her, that you're just using her for her connection to Jamie Peters. How's that supposed to make her feel?"

Lila got up and flicked her hair back with a perfectly manicured hand. "Don't be so concerned, Liz. I'm sure she's used to it. Personally, I can't wait to spend a little more time with Andrea. Maybe she and Jamie can fix me up with someone, and we can double-date. Someone like Bruce Springsteen."

"Yeah. You'll play that instrument of yours for him, and that'll be the end of that relationship," Jessica muttered.

"I've heard enough. Enid, let's get out of here." Elizabeth pushed her tray back in disgust.

Elizabeth felt terrible about the rumor. She knew it couldn't possibly be true. There was no way Andrea could be involved—that way—with Jamie Peters. If she was living with him, he must be her father. That was the only logical explanation.

But deep inside, an uncomfortable little voice in Elizabeth couldn't help but ask, *Then why didn't Andrea tell us? Why keep her identity a secret, unless she really does have something to hide?*

*   *   *

Andrea shifted uncomfortably on the deck chair near the pool and reached for what must have been the second box of tissues that afternoon. She had not had a cold like this in a long time, and it was making her feel terrible. Nothing helped, not even baking in the sun, her father's remedy for everything.

There was only one positive aspect to spending the day at home with a lousy cold, and that was having some time to herself to do some thinking. Andrea had been so busy since they had moved in that she hadn't been able to get much perspective on their new life.

This time everything would be different. Her father had promised her that. They had made a deal. This time they were settling in, building a home together.

Her father hadn't understood why she had been so insistent on keeping her identity a secret. "Why not just tell people? They're going to find out sooner or later," he had said.

But Andrea had stuck to her plan. "You don't know what it's like. The second people find out I'm your daughter, that's *all* I am. I want to have real friends, people who like me for myself," she had argued.

The great thing about her father was that he understood. He might be a big star, but when it came to the little things, he was amazingly sensitive. He knew how hard it had been on Andrea, moving so often, spending so much time traveling or staying with friends or relatives while he went on tour. It was hard trying to be a regular family, just the two of them. *If only Mom had lived* . . .

But Andrea had learned the hard way not to spend too long thinking about "ifs." Her mother had not lived. It *was* just the two of them, and they had had to make a home the best they could. Now that Andrea was grown up enough to be able to tell her father what she wanted and needed, she knew things would be better. And her father was getting sick of the "star" stuff too. He had told her before they moved out to Sweet Valley that he was finally ready for a real home. Home-cooked meals instead of restaurants and room service. A community, neighbors, the whole works.

What amazed Andrea was how happy she had been since they moved. Back in New York, she wondered if she would ever fit in and have a normal life. Now, to her absolute delight, she was discovering that the simplest things were the ones that meant the most. Having friends who liked her for herself, friends like Elizabeth and Enid. And Nicholas. Just thinking about Nicholas made her forget her cold. They were supposed to get together this week sometime, maybe see a movie. These were the things that made her happy. Not being the center of attention because of her father.

And her father seemed happier, too. He had not said much about the film contract his agent was working on, but she guessed that would come soon. So far, he seemed to like Sweet Valley as much as she did.

Deep down, Andrea was still afraid her father would start to feel restless and want to move on. But he had promised, hadn't he? There was no way he would let her down. Not now. Not when Sweet Valley was really beginning to feel like home.

Andrea swung her legs over the deck chair. Her throat hurt, and she had a feeling this was as good an excuse for ice cream as she would ever have.

She slipped through the sliding glass doors into the cool house. It was quiet, and she thought she heard her father's footsteps in the den. Then the phone rang, and she heard him pick it up.

Andrea helped herself to ice cream and sat

on one of the high stools in the kitchen. Her father's voice seemed closer now, and she realized he was using the mobile phone. He must be wandering back and forth in the living room. "Leo, listen," she heard him say.

Leo was her father's agent. Andrea's ears pricked up. Maybe they were finalizing the film contract. Once that contract was signed, she could count on staying in Sweet Valley for a long, long time.

"I don't know. It sounds good, but Andrea's got her heart set on sticking around," her father continued.

Andrea froze. Obviously, he thought she was still outside. She could feel her heart pound as he continued.

"Yeah, I know it's an incredible deal. And I love the idea of an Italian tour, Leo. But I told you. . . ." His voice trailed off. "OK, OK, Leo. Calm down. Get me the details and I'll think about it. Are you happy now?"

Andrea felt as if she had had the wind knocked out of her. Did this mean her father was seriously considering another tour? But he had promised! They'd made a deal!

She knew she should confront him, tell him exactly what she had heard. But Andrea could not bring herself to do it. Maybe if she just pretended she had never heard, it would all just go away.

Andrea had always dreaded the moment when her father turned to her with that mixture of concern and excitement and told her it was time to be moving on. This time, she knew she just could not bear it. And she was not going to let it happen, either. Whatever it took, Andrea was going to build a life for herself in Sweet Valley.

She wasn't going to ask her father what Leo had said. Even if he did go on tour, she wasn't going with him. This was her home now, and this was where she was going to stay.

Ten

"You're sure you're feeling well enough to go to school?" Jamie asked Andrea on Wednesday morning.

Andrea nodded. "I've got enough cold medicine with me to cure an army. And anyway, I don't want to get behind in any of my classes."

Andrea was feeling a little uncomfortable about not having told her father what she'd heard. She couldn't meet his eyes, and she could tell her father knew something was bothering her. They were usually very open with each other. Maybe her father thought she was acting strangely because of her cold.

It would be a relief to get to school and see

Elizabeth and Enid again. Even though she'd been away just one day, she had missed them.

And Nicholas, too. If she was feeling better, she really wanted to meet him somewhere that evening.

But to her disappointment, Andrea didn't make it to school early enough to see either Elizabeth or Enid. She had to rush straight to her first-period class.

Amy Sutton, who had not had much to say to Andrea since she had been introduced to the class by Mr. Jaworski, was all smiles this morning.

"Hi, Andrea! How *are* you?" Amy jumped out of her seat to come closer and talk. "Isn't it *the worst* missing school because of a cold? Do you need notes from yesterday?" Her gray eyes were full of solicitous concern. "I could get them for you and bring them by your house."

"No, I think I'm OK. But thanks." Andrea was a little confused. Since when was Amy Sutton so interested in her?

"You know, a bunch of us are having a party this weekend, kind of a last-minute thing," Amy continued. "If you'd like to come—"

Mr. Jaworski signaled that class was beginning, and Amy had to return to her seat. "I'll call you," she hissed as she gave Andrea a conspiratorial wink.

Andrea mustered a smile. Well, Amy had struck her as a little high strung. Maybe she had strange mood swings or something.

But mood swings couldn't explain the way Caroline Pearce and Sandra Bacon acted toward her in her second-period class. The two girls were whispering together when Andrea walked into the room. Then the whispering stopped, and both girls turned beet red and looked away from Andrea in complete embarrassment.

After class, Caroline sidled up to her. "Hi, Andrea. I noticed you weren't in class yesterday."

"I had a cold."

"Oh, *a cold*." There was something strangely insinuating about Caroline's tone, and Andrea didn't like it.

"I love your sweater," Caroline added, tagging along behind Andrea as she started walking toward her next class.

"Thanks," Andrea said, her confusion deepening.

Caroline was unshakable. She was waiting for Andrea after her next class and tried to extract a promise from her that they would eat lunch together. When Andrea told her she wasn't sure if she felt well enough to eat anything, Caroline looked hurt. "You know, people who know me think I'm a really good listener. They think I'm the sort of friend you can really confide in."

Andrea shook her head as she watched the redhead bound off down the hall. "What's going on here?" she muttered to herself. Had someone found out about her father somehow?

Three girls Andrea didn't know walked toward her, arms linked. When they saw Andrea, they put their heads together and giggled.

Andrea could feel her face burn with embarrassment and anger. This was exactly what had happened in her private school in New York. Everywhere she went, people had made such a big deal out of it. She was never Andrea, she was always Jamie Peters's daughter.

Andrea felt her eyes filling with tears. She could still remember, as if it were yesterday, the painful moment when she had found out that her supposed best friend in the world, Diana Cushing, had only been using her to get close to her father.

The stuff with Diana was ancient history, two years old now, but it still hurt. They had been in ninth grade together in a school in Boston.

Diana was the only girl in the whole school Andrea had trusted. They had told each other all their fears and secrets and became extremely close. And when Andrea found out that Diana's mother was a reporter for an entertainment magazine, she hadn't thought anything of it. She was used to a world in which everyone did some sort of media work. But eventually the truth had come out: Diana was friends with Andrea only because her mother wanted to get close to Jamie Peters. After her mother had finally gotten the story she wanted, Diana dropped Andrea with a thud that really brought her down to earth.

Since then, Andrea had given up all illusions of being friends with anyone who knew she was Jamie Peters's daughter. She knew now there was only one way to have a legitimate friendship. And that was to hide her real identity.

Just look at the way Amy Sutton and Caroline Pearce had been trying to kiss up to her that morning! They didn't care one bit about Andrea for her own sake. Had they paid any attention to her before? No way!

No, it was obvious. Somehow her secret had gotten out. The question was, how? Andrea had done everything possible to cover her tracks. No one knew where she lived, no one had ever seen her coming or going. She hadn't let her guard down once, not for a second, not even with Nicholas.

So how had they figured out that she was Jamie Peters's daughter?

By lunch hour, Andrea was convinced that someone had let her secret out of the bag. Everywhere she looked, people seemed to be whispering and staring at her. A few girls she didn't even know tried to sit with her at lunch, and Andrea had the miserable sense that what had happened in New York was happening here all over again.

So much for having her own friends, her own identity.

To her relief, she saw Enid and Elizabeth seated on the other side of the cafeteria. "Excuse me," she muttered, getting up and barely looking at the girls who had sat down beside her.

Elizabeth and Enid were deep in conversation and didn't see her as she approached. Andrea swallowed. This was the part she dreaded. Had Elizabeth and Enid heard the news? Would they treat her differently now that they knew?

"Andrea, hi!" Elizabeth said, greeting her with a big smile.

"How's your cold? Are you feeling better?" Enid asked.

Exactly as if nothing had changed! Andrea felt more confused than ever. She pulled up a chair, her mind buzzing. What should she do? Should she tell them the truth right now and explain why she had wanted to keep her identity a secret?

But before she could even turn the question over in her mind, Lila Fowler came bounding up to the table. "Andrea Slade, you are *exactly* the girl I have been looking for!" She pulled out a chair and sat down.

Enid and Elizabeth exchanged worried glances.

"Hi, Lila." Something about the look on Lila's face told Andrea that trouble was coming.

"Listen, I've been talking to Jessica and Amy about this, and they think it's nervy of me to ask you for a favor. But I feel as if we know each other pretty well. Don't you think so?" Lila demanded.

Andrea inhaled deeply and said nothing. Elizabeth and Enid were watching her closely.

"I've been taking music lessons from Max Sharpe. Have you heard of him?"

Andrea shook her head. "No, I haven't."

"He's wonderful," Lila informed her. "And

thanks to him, I've gotten really serious about an instrument called the marimba. It's African—but I'm sure you know all about it," she added slyly. "Knowing as much as you must about everything musical."

Andrea hated this. People making all sorts of assumptions about her because of her father. She wanted to escape. But she knew she couldn't keep running. She had to stick this out, no matter how she felt.

"I've never heard of the marimba," she said quietly, dreading what Lila was about to say.

"Well, seeing as you're—*you know*. I thought you might be able to ask Jamie Peters a favor for me." Lila tossed back her hair. "I wouldn't be asking if I didn't happen to think that I'm really good. But you know the music industry," she added coyly. "Who you know matters as much as how good you are."

Andrea's mouth was set. "Yes, I suppose you could say that." She wished Lila would just disappear into thin air. This was *exactly* the kind of thing she hated most.

Elizabeth cleared her throat. "Lila, I don't really think—"

But Lila cut her off. "Come on. We're all grownups, right? Why pretend?"

Andrea reached for a tissue. On top of these

aggravations, her cold was bothering her, too. "Lila, what is it, exactly, that you want?"

"I want you to set up an audition for me with Jamie. Nothing fancy, just a chance to let him hear what I sound like. Maybe when he cuts a new album—who knows? He might need a marimba player."

Even after a lifetime of dealing with this sort of behavior, Andrea still didn't know what to say in these situations. "I don't think that's a very good idea," she managed at last.

Lila was getting angry. "Come on, Andrea. Are you trying to say you don't have any sway over him?"

"That isn't the point," Andrea said coldly.

"Maybe you don't," Lila added with a pout. "Maybe he doesn't even listen to you. Although if I were you, that would bother me. A lot. After all, you *are* his girlfriend. Doesn't he always claim in his songs and interviews that he'd do *anything* for you?"

Andrea stared at Lila. At first, she thought she hadn't heard her right. Then she started to laugh.

"What's so funny?" Lila snapped. "Don't try to wriggle out of this one either, Andrea! We all know the truth now, so don't think you can deny it."

"What's the 'truth,' Lila?" Andrea asked, her

laughter subsiding and her anger taking over. "That Jamie Peters is my *boyfriend*?"

The scorn and incredulity in Andrea's voice seemed to silence Lila. For a long minute, Andrea watched her waver. But Lila couldn't bear it. Her curiosity got the best of her.

"Well, isn't he?" she asked.

Andrea got to her feet. She could feel a dull throbbing in her head. Answering Lila right then was a little bit like answering every kid who'd ever wanted to know, her whole life, who Jamie Peters was to her. She told Lila something she had wanted to say for so long but had never had the nerve to do. "Lila, listen to me. It's *none of your business* who Jamie Peters is to me!"

Lila's mouth dropped open. She didn't say a word.

"I've got to get out of here," Andrea muttered. She got to her feet and stomped off through the crowded lunchroom.

"Andrea, wait a second," Elizabeth called after her. But Andrea wouldn't turn back. She needed to be alone.

"Very tactful, Lila," Enid observed, watching Andrea rush off through the lunchroom.

"I agree. You have such a delicate touch," Elizabeth said with heavy irony.

Lila shook her head. "It isn't my fault she's so sensitive. How's she ever going to have a successful relationship with a rock star if she can't handle a few innocent little question?"

"Lila, what makes you still think Jamie Peters is Andrea's boyfriend?" Elizabeth demanded. "Didn't her reaction right now make you reconsider, or are you so sure you're always right?"

Lila got to her feet, an imperious expression on her face. "You two just don't recognize a cover-up when you see one. Of course she denied it. What else is she going to do? Admit to everyone that she's living with a big star like Jamie? After all, she's only a junior in high school. What if the teachers found out?"

Elizabeth shook her head. "Believe what you want, Lila. Only do me a favor. Quit spreading rumors till you know the truth."

Lila swung her long hair back over one shoulder. "Thanks for the advice, Liz. I'll keep it in mind."

Her voice was dripping with sarcasm. And before Elizabeth could say another word, she was gone.

Eleven

"Nice going, Lila," Jessica complained later that afternoon when Lila told her what had happened with Andrea at lunchtime. "Now you've blown it! I thought we agreed you would bring up the audition when the time was right. Not just blast the poor girl with it."

Lila made a face. "She's just another stuck-up star's girlfriend. She wasn't one little bit interested in trying to help me."

Jessica couldn't even pay attention to the great clothes that were on sale at the little boutique Lila had taken her to. She was too incensed at the thought of losing the chance of a friendship with Andrea Slade.

It was all Lila's fault. If Jessica had been the one to see Andrea first, she knew she would have handled everything perfectly. A couple of slick references to Jamie's latest album, a few compliments, and before you could say *Pride*, Jessica and Andrea would have been fast friends.

"You've blown it for all of us."

Lila picked up the sleeve of a yellow silk blouse. "Come on, Jess! I didn't blow it. Andrea was just a little ticked off because we saw through her disguise. She'll come around sooner or later. Once she wakes up out of whatever daze she's in, she'll realize that there are better people to be friends with than Enid Rollins."

"Watch it," Jessica said. It was alright for *her* to disapprove of Elizabeth's friendships, but family loyalty ran deep. And right now she was *not* in the mood to hear her twin's friend criticized, even indirectly.

"I'm sick of the whole thing, anyway," Lila continued, moving on to the next rack of clothes. "Who needs Andrea's help? Jamie will probably get sick of her and throw her out before too long. And no matter what, I've *got* to angle for an audition with him. Now that

I've finally discovered my true calling, I don't want to waste any more time."

"Right," Jessica said sarcastically. "So the way you see things, Jamie's going to dump Andrea, hire you as his star marimba player, and then you two will live happily ever after?"

"Something like that," Lila said blithely.

"This place is too expensive. I'm going outside for some fresh air," Jessica said crossly. Without waiting for Lila, she stomped out of the boutique into the brilliant sunshine.

The boutique, called Mata Hari's, was at the intersection of two main streets downtown. Jessica leaned back against the stucco wall of the shop, watching people hurrying to and fro. It was five o'clock, and people were getting out of work. It calmed her down a little to hang out for a while and watch them.

"Jessica!"

Nicholas Morrow was coming out of the Flower Shoppe across the street, his arms full of beautiful blue flowers.

Jessica waved back at him, but he was already hurrying across the street to say hello.

"Hi, Nicholas. Those are gorgeous. Who are they for?"

"A new friend," Nicholas said, grinning happily. "Actually, you probably know her. You

120

always know everyone, and she's in your grade. Andrea Slade." Nicholas beamed down at the flowers.

Jessica's eyebrows shot up. "Really?" What was Nicholas doing buying flowers for Andrea?

"She's had a cold, and I wanted to get something to cheer her up. I'm meeting her for tea in about half an hour." He looked at the flowers critically. "They're hydrangeas. Do you like them? It was hard finding something blue. Blue's Andrea's favorite color," he added.

Jessica stared at him. He really sounded lovesick! "Listen, Nicholas," she began.

Just then Lila burst out of the boutique, clutching a parcel. "Nicholas! Nice flowers," she exclaimed, taking the whole scene in with one quick glance. "Who are they for?"

"They're for Andrea," Jessica said before Nicholas could answer. She tried as hard as she could to make her expression convey a warning to Lila. But Lila didn't notice. "What a waste. I hope you don't have a crush on that girl, Nicholas," Lila said pityingly.

"Well, as a matter of fact, I *do* like her. She and I have gone out a few times and I think she's a lot of fun," Nicholas said, looking a little upset by Lila's remark.

121

"Great. So she's a two-timer on top of everything else," Lila said with a snort.

"What do you mean, two-timer?" Nicholas's face was begining to turn red.

"Lila doesn't mean anything." Jessica put her hand on Lila's arm and started to steer her away.

But there was no stopping Lila. "You mean you've been going out with Andrea and you don't even know she's living with Jamie Peters?" She shook her head. "You poor fool! Why is it all the nice guys get jerked around by girls like Andrea?"

Nicholas stared at her. "Andrea? Living with Jamie Peters? The rock star, Jamie Peters?"

"That's right," Lila said crisply. "And don't let her tell you otherwise because we happen to have seen them together over at the Kitterby place. That's where they live. And Andrea was all *over* him."

Nicholas looked horrified. "I don't believe it. No wonder she's been so weird every time I've tried to find out where she lived," he said slowly.

"It figures. She wouldn't want you to know, of course," Lila concurred.

"But why would Andrea be going out with Nicholas if she's supposedly in love with Jamie

Peters?'' Jessica asked. Nicholas looked more upset than ever, and she added quickly, "I don't mean that against *you*, Nicholas. It's just—well, if she's living with this guy, she must be pretty serious about him. So why—''

"You don't know anything about stars, Jessica,'' Lila said condescendingly. "Who knows? Maybe Andrea's insecure. Maybe she needs more than one man.'' She turned to Nicholas and patted him consolingly on the arm. "I'm just glad we got to you in time.''

"Yeah,'' Nicholas muttered. He looked numb and confused. "Here,'' he said, thrusting the flowers into Lila's arms. "You might as well take these. No point wasting them on someone who's probably just using me, anyway.''

Lila took the flowers. "Thanks, Nicholas. These are gorgeous!''

Jessica waited until Nicholas was out of earshot before she said anything to her friend. "Li, do you think that was really a good idea?''

Lila sniffed the flowers appreciatively. "Jess, since when are you so *sensitive*?'' She shook her head. "Nicholas Morrow ought to be grateful to me for the rest of his life. I saved him from making a huge mistake. To tell you the truth, I think he ought to send *me* flowers every day for a month, after what I've done for him!''

Jessica didn't respond. Suddenly she had an uneasy feeling in her stomach. What if *they* were the ones who had made a huge mistake?

Andrea was ten minutes late meeting Nicholas at the Fairmont, a lovely inn overlooking the marina that was famous for its afternoon teas. She had come early to the marina to be by herself for a while. Stupidly, she had forgotten a watch, and when she got to the inn, she was surprised to see the time.

"I'm meeting someone," she told the hostess. "A guy. He's tall, dark haired, really cute," she added. "His name is Nicholas Morrow. Is he here already?"

The hostess took an envelope out of the appointment book. "He came by about twenty minutes ago. He left this for you."

Andrea took the envelope, disappointment washing over her. She had really been looking forward to seeing Nicholas. She wanted to tell him what had happened today, to tell him the truth about her father and to ask his advice. That was one of the things she had been wrestling with that afternoon, and she was certain now it was essential to let him know who she was before he found out from someone else. Why hadn't he kept their date?

She sat down on a small couch in the front hall of the inn and tore open the letter.

"Dear Andrea," it began.

I'm sorry I couldn't meet you in person, but I don't really feel up to facing you right now. I think you'll understand how shocked I was when I ran into some people who know you from school, and they told me you were living with Jamie Peters. Why didn't you tell me, Andrea? I thought there was something really special between us. The last thing in the world I'd have ever imagined is that you could be involved with another guy. Now that I know the truth, I feel like an idiot. It's pretty hard being the last to know.

"I don't believe this," Andrea whispered, looking up from the letter, her eyes blurred with tears. What had started as a ridiculous misunderstanding had snowballed into a complete disaster. So someone had actually told Nicholas she was Jamie Peters's girlfriend! How could they!

You didn't tell Lila the truth, a voice inside her

said. *You were angry, you mocked her, but you didn't tell her the truth. If you had, maybe this wouldn't have happened.*

Her eyes swam with tears. She could imagine what Nicholas must have thought when he heard that awful rumor. All the good times between them must have been wiped out in an instant. *Now he thinks I'm a liar—and even worse.*

Andrea folded the letter and put it back into the envelope. She didn't know what to do. But she knew one thing. She could not go home and face her father until this whole wretched mess blew over.

Elizabeth and Jessica were in Elizabeth's bedroom, working together on their English homework when the telephone rang.

"I'll get it. It's for me." Jessica practically knocked her twin over as she lunged for the receiver.

Elizabeth frowned. "It's eight-thirty. Todd's supposed to be calling."

But Jessica already had the phone. "Hello," she said breathlessly. "Who?" she gasped a second later. Her eyebrows shot up so far, Elizabeth thought she must have gotten an electric shock. "Uh—yes—I mean, no—this is her

126

sister. . . . But *I* could talk to you. . . . Unh-huh. . . . Oh, I see. Yes." Jessica covered the receiver with one hand. She was trembling with excitement. "It's Jamie Peters. He wants to talk to you!"

Elizabeth was startled. "Jamie Peters wants to talk to *me*?" She jumped up and reached for the phone.

"I don't believe it," Jessica moaned. "You don't even like his music that much, and he wants to talk to *you*! Of all the rotten luck!"

"Hello," Elizabeth said, surprised by how nervous she felt to be talking to such a big star.

"Elizabeth, you don't know me. My name is Jamie Peters." His voice was so natural and down-to-earth that Elizabeth instantly felt at ease. "I happen to be the father of a classmate of yours. A friend, I think. Andrea Slade."

Elizabeth felt enormous relief wash over her. "You're Andrea's *father*?" she repeated. She was immediately angry with herself for having doubted Andrea even the tiniest little bit.

Jessica looked as if a bomb had just exploded in front of her. "No way!" she cried as she clapped her hand over her mouth.

"Yes. I think she didn't want anyone at her new school to know because in the past it's been a source of a lot of pain for her, actually."

127

He cleared his throat. "I'm very sorry to be calling you like this, but I found your telephone number on Andrea's desk, and I've heard her mention your name a number of times. Yours, and a girl named Enid. Is that right? Her number's here, too."

"Yes, Enid. That's right."

"Frankly, I don't know who else to turn to. We're new here, and I haven't met many people yet. Anyway, Andrea never came home from school today. At first I wasn't that concerned. She's very independent, and I just assumed she was out with friends. I was hoping she might be with you."

"No." Elizabeth felt a bit alarmed. "No, I'm sorry, but she isn't."

"Oh. Could she be at Enid's? I thought you might have some idea—"

"I can call Enid," Elizabeth said rapidly, "but I don't think Andrea's with her."

"She always calls, or at least leaves a message for me, if she's going to miss dinner." Jamie Peters sounded increasingly anxious. "She doesn't know this town very well, and I'm pretty worried. Do you have any idea where she could be?"

"I'll tell you what. I can call Enid, and Nicholas Morrow. One of them may have an idea,"

Elizabeth said. "Maybe we could drive around and look for her. She may just be out taking a walk or something."

"If you could, that would be great. Why don't you come over here if you can't find her. We can all try to figure out something. I hate to call the police and get them involved if she's not in danger, but I'm very worried about her."

"We'll start looking for her right away," Elizabeth promised.

Jamie gave her directions to his house, and Elizabeth hung up. Elizabeth was about to go downstairs to tell her parents where she was going, but Jessica stopped her. "Listen, Liz, before you go, I think there's something I'd better tell you."

"Jessica, not now! I don't have time!" Elizabeth exclaimed.

"It's urgent, Liz. I don't know where Andrea is, but I think I may know part of the reason why she didn't come home. And I've got to tell you before you call Nicholas and ask him to help you."

Twelve

Elizabeth drove the Fiat up the long winding drive to the Morrows' house. She had already called Enid and told her they would be over in five or ten minutes. She wanted to pick up Nicholas first. She wanted a chance to be alone with him before they started to look for Andrea. All she had said to Nicholas on the phone was that she had something urgent to tell him about Andrea.

Nicholas was outside, pacing back and forth, when Elizabeth arrived. "Thank God you're here. I've been going nuts!" he exclaimed, yanking open the door to the car and jumping in. "What's going on? Is Andrea in trouble?"

Elizabeth started down the driveway. "Lis-

130

ten, Jessica told me what happened this afternoon, what Lila told you. You must've been pretty upset."

"Yeah, I was," Nicholas said quietly. "But that doesn't change the fact that I care about her. If she's hurt—"

"Nicholas, listen to me for a second. Andrea isn't Jamie Peters's girlfriend."

"She isn't?"

"No. Jamie Peters is her *father*."

Nicholas was shocked. "You mean she's . . . and I told her . . ." He shook his head. "What a jerk I am! I should've talked to Andrea myself instead of just standing her up like that. She's never going to forgive me for believing that kind of gossip!"

Elizabeth turned the Fiat toward Enid's house. "Is that what happened? You stood her up? Nicholas, do you think that would have been enough to keep Andrea from coming home tonight?"

Nicholas tapped his leg nervously. "That isn't all. I left a note for her at the place where we were supposed to meet, telling her exactly how I felt about having been betrayed. She must've freaked out when she read it."

Elizabeth sighed. "So maybe that was it. On top of everyone at school treating her so strangely, your reaction must've been the last straw."

"Where is she, Liz? Tell me what's going on," Nicholas pleaded.

Elizabeth drove up the Rollinses' driveway and put the car in park. "I don't know where she is, Nicholas. That's just the problem. According to her father, she hasn't come home from school yet. She could be anywhere."

Enid ran out to meet them. "Am I going to fit?" she asked. "Maybe we'd better take my mom's car. If we find Andrea—"

Nicholas looked tense. "Don't say 'if,' Enid. We've *got* to find her. I'm not giving up until we've combed this entire town!"

"We'll find her, Nicholas." Elizabeth tried to sound reassuring. She just wished she felt as confident as she sounded.

"Where to?" Enid asked, putting the car in drive.

"I don't know." Elizabeth frowned. "Should we just try circling through town once?"

"It's as good a plan as any," Enid said. They drove in silence through town. Most of the shops and restaurants were closing, and the street were rapidly becoming deserted.

"Do you think she could be at school? Maybe just kind of hanging out?" Elizabeth wondered.

"Not after the scene there today. She wouldn't want to go back there," Enid replied. "Oh, I almost forgot. Jamie called me before you two came over. He said that he was leaving a message with his sister Donna, in L.A. If Andrea turns up there, she'll call him."

Nicholas looked grim. "I hope she didn't go all the way to L.A. alone this late."

"I don't think so. She probably just wanted to be alone and think for a while," Elizabeth mused. "The question is, where?"

Nicholas snapped his fingers. "I've got it. Enid, turn around," he commanded. "Take a left at the light and head down to the marina."

"The marina?"

"Trust me." Nicholas looked excited. "If Andrea's anywhere nearby, she'll be there. I don't know why I didn't think of it sooner."

They drove the rest of the way in silence. For Elizabeth's part, that silence was an uneasy one. She was relieved when they finally reached the marina. At least they could get out of the car and *do* something.

"Down there, near the pier!" Nicholas called, slamming the car door shut and loping ahead. "She's got to be there."

Enid grabbed a flashlight from the glove compartment, and she and Elizabeth followed closely behind. It was pitch black, and the sailboats looked ghostly in the water. Elizabeth shivered a little. The ocean looked so much more awesome in the darkness!

Nicholas took the flashlight Enid handed him and switched it on. "Andrea?" he called.

"Wait," Enid said, stopping short. "I think I heard something over there."

Nicholas pointed the flashlight in the direction on the dock, and the circle of light picked out a huddled form.

"Andrea!" Nicholas hollered.

Elizabeth grabbed Enid's arm. The girl on the dock was turning around, obviously surprised.

It was Andrea.

"Andrea, I'm so sorry," Nicholas cried, running toward her.

Andrea stood and stared at him uncertainly. "Wh-what are you guys doing here?" she choked out.

"I blew it. I made a total fool out of myself, and I'm sorry. Do you think you can possibly forgive me?" Nicholas asked her.

Andrea shivered and rubbed her arms. She looked from Elizabeth to Enid to Nicholas.

"How did you find me here?" she asked slowly.

"Nicholas knew you'd be here," Elizabeth told her.

Andrea turned to him. "I don't get it, Nicholas. One minute you leave me a note saying you never want to see me again, and the next—"

"Listen, I ran into some friends downtown on my way to the inn. I had these beautiful blue flowers for you." Nicholas looked miserable. "I told them how I felt about you, and they told me I was a fool. They said you were Jamie Peters's girlfriend. I'm so sorry, Andrea. I should never have believed what they said."

Andrea sighed. "I guess the truth's out now, right? You all know I'm his daughter."

"We know," Enid said softly. "And to tell you the truth, it doesn't matter one bit."

"Yeah," Andrea said, "that's what you say now, but just wait awhile."

"Andrea, who cares who your father is? I'm just so glad Jamie Peters isn't your boyfriend!" Nicholas looked at her more closely. "You're not ashamed of him, are you?"

"No!" she burst out. "It's just— Oh, I don't know, it's just kind of hard being the daughter of a big star. People always treat you differently. They want to be friends with you just

135

because your father is famous. Not because they like you."

"Don't you have a little more faith in us than that?" Enid asked her.

"Of course I do! But I'm still scared. I guess it's because I've gotten burned in the past, that's all." She turned to Nicholas. "I owe you an apology, too. I hid so much from you, and you could tell I wasn't being honest about where I lived, who I was. I'm not saying I can understand how you could believe I was *living* with my dad—that way." She laughed. "I mean, he's young for a dad, but he's a little too old to have a teenage girlfriend! But I have to admit, I did my part to confuse the issue."

"We'd better go. Your dad is frantic. Can we drive you home now?"

Andrea nodded. "Yeah, I'll pick up my car tomorrow. All these revelations have really tired me out." She let Nicholas put his arm around her as they headed toward Enid's car.

"I've got another question, Andrea," Elizabeth said as they started back toward her father's house. "I can see why you wouldn't have wanted to call any of us after what happened in school today. But why not call your father?"

Andrea was holding Nicholas's hand very tightly. "I don't know all the reasons. But I've been scared to tell him how I'm feeling. I'm afraid my father is about to agree to do a European tour. That means moving again. At the very least I'd have to move up to L.A. to be with my Aunt Donna. I guess I'm pretty scared and angry when I think about that."

Nicholas squeezed Andrea's hand. "He's really thinking of going on tour? But you two just got here!"

"I know." Andrea sighed. "And we made a promise to each other. This time we were going to make a real home. With real friends," she added. "But I overheard him talking to Leo, his agent, on the phone the other day. It sounded as if he was pretty serious about going."

Nobody knew what to say. It seemed incredibly unfair. After everything Andrea had been through, having to pick up and move again seemed far too cruel.

"Maybe he'll change his mind," Elizabeth said. "After tonight, after he sees how upset you are."

"I hope so." Andrea tightened her hand around Nicholas's. "Because to tell you the truth, I don't think I could bear to leave. No matter what my father does, I'm going to stay in Sweet Valley."

Thirteen

"I'm not so sure this is a good idea," Jessica whispered to Lila. "Haven't we already gotten ourselves into enough trouble?"

It was late Wednesday evening. After Jamie Peters had called for Elizabeth, Jessica just couldn't sit still. She felt as if she *had* to do something, and part of what she had to do was to let Lila know what a mess they had gotten themselves into.

Telling her parents that she had to help find Andrea, Jessica had convinced her mother to let her borrow her car. Ten minutes later she was at Lila's house, explaining what had happened earlier.

At first, Lila refused to believe her. Finally, she backed down and admitted she may have made a mistake. "But I don't see what the big deal is. Why didn't Andrea just tell me I was wrong? And why did she try to hide the fact that she's Jamie Peters's daughter?" Lila shook her head in amazement. "Frankly, if I were her, I'd be playing it up for all it's worth."

"Yeah, well, obviously she feels differently about it."

That was when Lila decided they *had* to go back to their lookout spot, just the two of them, for one last glimpse of Jamie Peters—and a chance to see any action firsthand.

"I don't know, Lila," Jessica said hesitantly. "Let's just stay out of this whole thing. I don't want to get in any more trouble."

"Well, if you're scared, I can just go myself," Lila said scornfully.

That quieted Jessica. She wasn't going to let Lila accuse her of backing out on anything. But ten minutes later, crouched down in the blackness behind the bushes, she wished she had followed her instincts.

"Hey," Lila said, grabbing her arm, "look!"

The back door was sliding open, and lights snapped on, illuminating the patio and pool. There was a confusion of happy voices, and through it all they could hear Jamie say, "Thank God you're OK, Andrea. I was so worried about you."

"I'm sorry, Dad. I know I should've called and left a message. But I just felt I had to get away from everything for a little while. I really needed to clear my head."

Jessica poked Lila. "See? She called him Dad. What more proof could you want?"

"Shhh," Lila said crossly.

Jessica repositioned herself to get a better view. Andrea was standing next to Nicholas, holding his hand. Elizabeth and Enid were right next to them.

Jamie pulled up some deck chairs. "Well, I think we have plenty of cause here for celebration. First off, let me just say how great it is to finally meet Andrea's new friends."

"It's great for us, too," Nicholas said, putting his arm around Andrea.

"It's important for me to know who Andrea's hanging around with," he added, grinning. "Especially since I just gave my agent a signed copy of a movie contract that is going to *force* us to stay here in Sweet Valley for at least a couple of years!"

Andrea let out a shriek. "Daddy, you're kidding me! You didn't!" She gave him a giant hug. "But what about that tour in Italy?" she asked, backing off suddenly.

"How did you know about that?"

Andrea looked embarrassed. "I, uh, sort of overheard you and Leo the other day on the phone. When I was home sick," she added uncomfortably.

"Why didn't you just ask me about it? I called Leo back and told him to forget it." Jamie shook his head. "You and I had a deal. I wasn't going to quit on you, babe."

Nicholas laughed. "It's easy to see how rumors and misunderstandings get started."

Andrea sighed. "I feel like such a jerk. I should've come to you right away, Dad. I should've told you how upset I was, thinking you might go on tour and that we'd have to sell this beautiful house."

"I don't blame you for being scared to talk to me about it. You were probably afraid I wouldn't keep my promise." Jamie hugged her again. "I just hope you realize I'm not going to let you down again. OK?"

Andrea nodded. "OK," she said softly. She turned to Nicholas. "I should've been more open with everyone. When I first heard those rumors that were circulating about my father and me—"

"What rumors?" Jamie asked.

Lila poked Jessica this time. But the poke was a little more forceful than it should have been. Jessica lost her balance and toppled forward into the calla lily bushes. "Lila, you idiot," she hissed, struggling to get back into a crouching position.

"Hey, what's that noise in the bushes?" Andrea exclaimed.

"Yeah, I heard it too." Jamie turned to face the bushes.

"Now what?" Jessica gasped.

"Run!" Lila cried in a stage whisper.

But neither of them managed to scramble out of the shrubs before Jamie and Nicholas were on top of them, yanking them onto the patio where Enid, Elizabeth, and Andrea stood gaping at them.

"I—uh—I'm sorry," Jessica stammered, staring in complete mortification at Jamie Peters. This wasn't exactly the way she had planned to meet her idol.

"Jessica, what on earth are you doing?" Elizabeth cried.

Jamie raised his eyebrows. "Sounds like you know these two."

"Yeah, we know them all right," Nicholas

said angrily. "The question is, what were they doing in the bushes?"

Lila brushed a piece of greenery out of her hair. With perfect composure, she put her hand out to shake Jamie's. "My name is Lila Fowler. I live a few doors down. Perhaps you've noticed our mansion, Fowler Crest? It's a real pleasure to meet you."

"Ordinarily, I'd say it's a pleasure, too. But I have to tell you, I'm not used to welcomes from neighbors at this time of night. And unless I'm mistaken, neighbors usually come in through the front door, not through the shrubs."

"We were too shy, sir," Lila lied blithely.

Jessica had to hand it to her. Lila was cool!

"Something tells me I know how those rumors got started now," Elizabeth said dryly. "Jess, how many nights of chores are you going to trade me for keeping this one a secret from Mom and Dad?"

Jamie looked from Jessica to Elizabeth. "Oh, I get it! No wonder you two look so familiar. You've got the same face!" he cried.

Lila turned to Andrea then. "Listen, we owe you an apology. That's really why we came over tonight," she added smoothly. "We're the ones to blame for telling people you and Jamie were involved. But we didn't mean to hurt anyone. Its just—well, Jessica happened to have seen you two together downtown, and we just assumed, you know.''

Jamie's confusion was growing more pronounced. "Wait a second. Could someone please tell me what's going on here? I feel like I've walked into a play in the third act.''

"Maybe I can,'' Nicholas said. "As far as I can tell, what happened is that Lila and Jessica somehow got the idea in their heads that you and Andrea . . . that Andrea was your girlfriend. And they told everyone at school. Am I right?''

"More or less,'' Jessica whispered, hanging her head.

"Wow. I should be flattered. You guys think I look that young!'' Jamie laughed.

"Well, all the star magazines always talk about your 'special girl.' And your songs, like 'Doing It All for You.' '' Jessica knew she was blabbing and wished she could disappear into the bushes again.

Jamie laughed. "Well, you've met my special girl. They don't come any more special than Andrea.''

"Yeah, I agree with that,'' Nicholas said fervently.

Andrea cleared her throat. "I wish I could

just tell you two that it's all OK, that I forgive you. But it's pretty rotten hearing stuff like that going around. Imagine how you'd feel if you were in my position."

"I'll tell you what," Lila said. "Jessica and I will *personally* guarantee that everyone at school will know the real truth about you and Jamie Peters. Will that help?"

"I guess so," Andrea said uncertainly. "Anyway, I've learned a lesson since I've been in Sweet Valley. It isn't worth keeping secrets. Somehow they always backfire."

Jamie smiled at his daughter. "Looks like you and I learned the same lesson. Here I was trying to keep the film contract a surprise for you, and all I did was to break your heart. And make you think I might be dragging you off to Italy!"

"Now that we're here," Jessica said, having regained her composure and unable to control herself any longer, "do we get to find out more about the movie you're making?"

Jamie laughed. "I don't think this is the best time. Do you realize it's almost eleven o'clock? Your parents are going to be as worried about you as I was about Andrea!"

"He's right. We should be going," Elizabeth agreed. Now that everything was resolved, she realized how tired she was.

"Before you go, let me just thank you two," Andrea said warmly. She put one hand on Enid's shoulder and the other on Elizabeth's. "Something tells me that the three of us are going to have a lot of fun together." She glanced shyly at Nicholas. "I feel as if I've made some *real friends* in Sweet Valley. People who care about me for who I am, not for who my father is."

"You know something? You're absolutely right," Elizabeth said, leaning forward to give Andrea a hug.

Jessica cleared her throat. "If we're going, we should go." Lila looked as if she were too enraptured with Jamie Peters to be anywhere close to leaving.

"Come on, Lila!" Jessica cried.

"You guys go ahead. I just have a quick question I have to ask Jamie."

Jessica groaned. Even as she walked through the patio door, she distinctly heard Lila pronouncing the word *marimba.*

"Well, I guess everything came out OK in the end," Elizabeth said to Enid as they sat in the Box Tree Café after school on Friday, having a cold drink and making plans for the weekend.

"Yeah. I'm so glad Andrea's going to be staying in Sweet Valley for a while," Enid said warmly. "Especially now that she's gotten over this stuff about her father. Everyone knows at school now, and it doesn't seem as if things are going to change very much."

"No," Elizabeth agreed. "I suppose there will always be a few jerks who'll try to use her because her father's famous. But by and large, I think her life is going to settle down pretty quickly now."

Enid took a sip of her soda. "I still laugh every time I remember the look on Jessica and Lila's faces when Jamie and Nicholas pulled them into the light!"

"Me too." Elizabeth giggled. "I'm trying to use that little story to my advantage. I've already coerced Jessica into doing all my chores this weekend!"

"The funniest thing is what's happened with Lila. I couldn't believe it when Andrea told us that her father wants to give Lila a bit part in the movie he's making!"

This piece of news had stunned everybody, particularly Jessica and Amy Sutton.

"Apparently she isn't that good. That's what Andrea told me, anyway. But Jamie thinks she might be perfect for a small comic role in the movie, as a marimba player! Lila's been telling everyone she's been discovered!" Elizabeth rolled her eyes.

"Yeah, she came out of the whole thing a little too well!"

The two girls laughed and chatted for a while before deciding to meet later that evening at a movie. Todd would be joining them, as well as Andrea and Nicholas.

"See you later." Elizabeth gave Enid an impulsive hug. "And thanks for introducing me to Andrea Slade. She's a terrific girl, and I may never have gotten to know her if it weren't for you."

Enid returned the hug and headed off. Elizabeth crossed the street to the spot where her Fiat was parked, still smiling as she went over the events of the past few weeks in her mind. She was so deep in thought that she didn't notice Skye Morrow, Nicholas's mother, coming out of small grocery store not far from the Fiat.

"Elizabeth!"

Elizabeth looked down the street. "Oh, Mrs. Morrow! I'm so sorry. I was in a daze," she admitted ruefully as they walked toward each other. "How are you?"

Mrs. Morrow certainly looked well, but then, Skye was a beautiful woman. She had been a fashion model before Nicholas and Regina were born, and her chiseled features were still absolutely striking. But her expression these days was mournful.

"I'm all right, Elizabeth. And I'm glad to see you. I have something for you. I was planning to call you about it this weekend."

"Really?"

"I know how close you were to Regina." Mrs. Morrow sighed heavily. "I often think about how dear a friend to her you were, how helpful you were when she was agonizing about going to Switzerland for the operations, and how sweet you were to her at school. She spoke so lovingly of you."

Elizabeth felt a lump forming in her throat. "I still can't believe it," she said softly. "It's so sad."

Mrs. Morrow steeled herself. "It's been extremely hard for all of us. To be honest, I didn't even have the strength to go through Regina's things. Not until just this past week. And that's when I found—well, it's something I'd like for you to have. I know Regina would've wanted you to have something of hers."

Elizabeth was deeply touched. "That means so much to me."

"I'll tell you what. If it's all right with you, I'll drop the package off tomorrow at your house."

"Thanks." Spontaneously, Elizabeth gave Mrs. Morrow a warm embrace. Everything about her, particularly her beauty and her delicacy, reminded her of Regina.

Elizabeth was extremely moved to think the Morrows wanted her to have a keepsake of Regina. Whatever it was, she knew she would cherish it. It would be as if part of Regina were still with her, something tangible to remind her of someone she still missed very deeply. She could hardly wait until the next day, when Mrs. Morrow's package would arrive.

What could Regina's mother want Elizabeth to have? Find out in Sweet Valley High #73, **REGINA'S LEGACY.**

MURDER AND MYSTERY STRIKES

America's favorite teen series has a hot new line of
Super Thrillers!

It's super excitement, super suspense, and super thrills as Jessica and Elizabeth Wakefield put on their detective caps in the new SWEET VALLEY HIGH SUPER THRILLERS! Follow these two sleuths as they witness a murder…find themselves running from the mob…and uncover the dark secrets of a mysterious woman. SWEET VALLEY HIGH SUPER THRILLERS are guaranteed to keep you on the edge of your seat!

YOU'LL WANT TO READ THEM ALL!

☐	27590	**BITTER RIVALS #29**	$2.95
☐	27558	**JEALOUS LIES #30**	$2.95
☐	27490	**TAKING SIDES #31**	$2.95
☐	27560	**THE NEW JESSICA #32**	$2.95
☐	27491	**STARTING OVER #33**	$2.95
☐	27521	**FORBIDDEN LOVE #34**	$2.95
☐	27666	**OUT OF CONTROL #35**	$2.95
☐	27662	**LAST CHANCE #36**	$2.95
☐	27884	**RUMORS #37**	$2.95
☐	27631	**LEAVING HOME #38**	$2.95
☐	27691	**SECRET ADMIRER #39**	$2.95
☐	27692	**ON THE EDGE #40**	$2.95
☐	27693	**OUTCAST #41**	$2.95
☐	26951	**CAUGHT IN THE MIDDLE #42**	$2.95
☐	27006	**HARD CHOICES #43**	$2.95
☐	27064	**PRETENSES #44**	$2.95
☐	27176	**FAMILY SECRETS #45**	$2.95
☐	27278	**DECISIONS #46**	$2.95
☐	27359	**TROUBLEMAKER #47**	$2.95
☐	27416	**SLAM BOOK FEVER #48**	$2.95
☐	27477	**PLAYING FOR KEEPS #49**	$2.95
☐	27596	**OUT OF REACH #50**	$2.95

Buy them at your local bookstore or use this page to order.

- - - - - - - - - - - - - - - - - - - -

Bantam Books, Dept. SVH2, 414 East Golf Road, Des Plaines, IL 60016

Please send me the items I have checked above. I am enclosing $_____
(please add $2.00 to cover postage and handling). Send check or money
order, no cash or C.O.D.s please.

Mr/Ms _____

Address _____

City/State _____ Zip _____

SVH2–11/89

Please allow four to six weeks for delivery.
Prices and availability subject to change without notice.